CW00664744

Burnt

A Marine Raiders Romance Book Three

Allyson Charles

To the extent that the image or images on the cover of this book depict a person or persons, such person or persons are merely models, and are not intended to portray any character or characters featured in the book.

Copyright © 2022 by Allyson Charles

ISBN-13: 978-1-944802-38-7

ISBN-10: 1-944802-38-X

All rights reserved. No part of this book may be reproduced in any form or by any means without the prior written consent of the Publisher, excepting brief quotes used in reviews.

Cover art by Dar Albert

Chapter One

THE CHERRIES ON HER little, white dress were driving him crazy. The small red fruit jiggled with each step she took, luring him forward, like a sailor after a siren.

Travis Kowalski was not the type of man to be lured. He did the tempting. The teasing. But the vision ahead of him, with her dark chocolate curls, her sexy sundress and curves that didn't quit, could have led him straight off a cliff with one little crook of her finger. She was a 1940s pin-up girl come to life, and like the servicemen that preceded him, he would have happily gone off to battle with a picture of her taped to his bunk.

His friend and fellow squad member, Chris Gunn, paused before yet another window. "What do you think of that bike?" Chris pointed to a bubble-gum pink monstrosity with a wide seat and handles that were just begging for an eight-year-old to attach ribbons to. The man was shopping for his girlfriend's birthday and had somehow convinced Travis to join him for the expedition.

Travis had thought he'd been invited as part of a rescue mission. To save his fellow Marine Raider from an afternoon of drudgery. After all, having each other's backs was what they did. But no, Chris didn't need rescuing. He'd needed an extra pair of hands to carry all the crap he was buying.

Travis shifted his weight off his sore leg. "I think you shop like a girl." His gaze flicked back to the woman, tracking her. She couldn't walk too far in those cherry-red heels. They were in Swansboro, North Carolina, a cutesy town not far from Camp Lejeune, the Marine base they were attached to. Tourists came here to shop and eat and take in the ocean breezes. They were nearing the edge of the downtown. The street dead-ended at the water only a couple of blocks up. Where was his siren heading?

Chris sighed. "I'm almost done. Now tell me what you think of the damn bike."

Travis thought his friend was pussy-whipped and had finally begun his descent into matching tattoos, his and her mani/pedis, and the ever-so-annoying couple who finishes each other's sentences.

Travis scratched his chest with his free hand. Two of his squad mates had finally found what they called the loves of their lives. He was happy for them, really, and maybe also the littlest bit jealous.

He darted a glance at cherry-woman. She was entering a store near the end of the street. He got one last look of a curvy ass before it disappeared.

Waking up with the same woman every day, someone you truly cared about? Well, the idea of that didn't suck.

Chris waved his hand in front of Travis's face, his shopping bags swinging. "Earth to Skee. Come in."

Travis knocked his hand away. "I think the bike is way too young for Sam. Unless it's a gag gift?"

"It's not for Sam." Chris turned back to peer through the window. "I want to get something for Maddie." Maddie was Sam's younger sister. Sam had custody of her, and after everything the girl had gone through, Chris had taken on a parental role. All of their friends felt protective toward the girl.

"Oh." Travis re-examined the bike. "It's still too young. Maddie will be going to college in a couple of years. And she'd hate pink."

Chris blew out a breath. "You're right. It's just, it will be *her* birthday in a couple of months, and I don't—"

"I'm sure they have other bikes." Travis backed away. The air fryer in the bag he was holding knocked into his leg, and he shut down a wince. He shoved the bag at his friend, who juggled everything in his arms to take it. "You go inside and look around. I'll meet you back here."

"Where are you going?"

Travis pointed at the building cherry-lady had disappeared into. "I have something of my own I want to pick up."

"*It's Your Jam*," Chris read the sign above the store's door, frowning. "But you don't eat sweets."

"I might be developing a taste." Travis saluted and turned for the shop.

"How much more walking are you going to do?" Chris shouted. "You know the doctor said—"

Travis cut him off with another salute, this time of the one-figured variety. He knew what the doctor said. And it was cute that after marching him to every damn candle, clothing, and knickknack shop in town, *now* Chris was concerned about how far he walked.

Travis hated his injury. More than the nagging ache that made it hard to sleep, he hated that he'd been grounded from joining his team on their last mission. But the pecker-checker said in another week or so Travis should have the green light to return to active.

He paused in front of *It's Your Jam*. The building's cream, slatboard front had a rustic look, and brightly-colored pyramids of jam were framed by both windows. A bell at the top of the door tinkled as he went inside, the sound drowned out by the raised voices and loud clatters coming from the open door at the back that must lead to a kitchen.

A pastry display stretched next to the counter and cash register, stacks of tarts, cupcakes, and cookies sitting atop pink and purple polka-dot doilies. Jars of jams and preserves spilled out from hutches and tables all around the room. A small eating area was set off to the side with three round wrought-iron tables with chairs squeezed around them.

The front room was deserted. Well, almost.

Travis tilted his head and peered under one of the tables. A young girl stared back at him, rolling a small ball between her equally small hands. She could have been anywhere between five and ten. Apart from once having been a child, Travis knew little about them.

Something else crashed in the back. A woman shrieked in frustration.

Travis glanced back at the girl. "Are you supposed to be here? Where's your mom?"

She pointed to the back room, dropping her marble in the process. She reached into a small mint-green bag for another glass ball.

"Huh." Travis scraped his palm across his jaw. His cherry woman was a mom. She and the girl had the same dark curls. The same heart-shaped face. He kind of hated himself for asking the question, but it had to be done. "Is your dad here, too?"

The pipsqueak shook her head. "I don't have a dad anymore. He died."

Travis blew out his cheeks. On the one hand, he was glad the woman was available. After watching those hips swing for five blocks, seeing the weary yet resolute expression on her face as she lifted it to the sun, it would hurt to have to turn around and leave now. On the other hand, what kind of dick was relieved a father was dead?

The shouts had tapered down to low murmurings. There was a call bell on the counter by the register. Travis supposed he should announce his presence. Instead he padded to the tables and squatted next to the girl.

If he was going to date a single mom, he should get her kid to like him.

And he wanted to date her mom very much.

"What's in those marbles?" he asked. Dark shapes lurked in the clear glass balls.

"My favorite animals." She held one up. "An owl." She pointed at another. "Octopus. Dolphin. And the best one ever...." She gave him a one-eyed squint before slowing holding her treasured marble up in her hand. "A unicorn."

"I'll be damned." There actually were small, carved animals within each marble. Travis had never seen such a thing.

"You're not supposed to swear," she told him solemnly.

Fuck. He was a Marine. Swearing was second nature. "Why don't we keep that our little secret?"

"And I'm not supposed to keep secrets with adults besides my mom."

Travis gripped the back of his neck. He couldn't argue with that rule. Hopefully, the little imp would forget about his language and not go telling tales to her mom.

"Can I see the unicorn more closely?" he asked, holding out his hand.

The girl frowned suspiciously. "I guess. I want it back though."

"Matilda, it's flash card time...." The woman in the cherry dress bustled out from the back. She stopped when she caught sight of Travis.

Up close, she was even more beautiful. Luminous skin. Red lips. A scarlet apron now covered part of her dress, the straps criss-crossing over her waist, emphasizing her hour-glass figure. He rose, just as Matilda released the marble. It plopped to the floor and slowly wove a path across the hardwood planks.

"I'm sorry." The woman tucked a loose curl behind her ear. "I didn't realize I had a customer. How can I help you?" She stepped forward.

Right onto the marble.

Her eyes flew wide as her foot shot out from under her. She windmilled her arms, but gravity was winning.

Travis leapt forward. He caught her only feet from the ground and pulled her close.

Her breasts heaved against his chest. She blinked, her long, dark lashes fluttering against her cheeks. Travis tried to keep his hands in PG places, but most of this woman's body was X-rated.

She clutched his shoulders, blinking as her fingers traced along the ridge of his trapezoid muscles. She sucked her lower lip into her mouth. It came out with a pop. "Oh, my," she breathed.

Travis pulled her tighter as he stood upright, letting himself enjoy every inch of contact. All his muscles quivered. It was like his body was a dowsing rod, directing him right to this woman. He'd never felt such an instant connection. An instant longing, that went deeper than any physical need.

He stared into her big, brown eyes, the air around them so charged it almost crackled.

Oh my, indeed.

Chapter Two

A TINGLE STARTED AT the base of Willow's spine and shivered its way up her back. Every inch of the man who held her was hard, except for his amber eyes, which twinkled softly. Her mind blanked, her body just enjoying being close to a man's when she hadn't had so much as a date in more than three years.

Daughter. Business. Decorum. The concepts forced their way into her head. It was that last one that had her pushing at his shoulders and stepping away, her cheeks heating.

She tucked an errant curl back. "Uh, thanks for the rescue."

And the man certainly looked like he knew how to conduct a rescue. Six foot something of solid muscle. The biceps stretching the arms of his black tee looked like they could probably do curls with her not-insubstantial body. His short brown hair had hints of highlights the color of her strawberry preserves. He had a strong jaw, blunt nose, and little lines around his eyes and mouth that spoke of someone who liked to laugh.

She couldn't remember the last time she'd laughed.

She turned her back on the stranger. Her eyes needed a break from all that hotness. "Matilda Rae Janna. You know better than to play with your marbles here. What if a customer had slipped on it?" The thought was like a bucket of ice water over her head. She was having enough problems with her jam shop. She didn't need a lawsuit.

Willow rubbed her ear. She also didn't want to see anyone get hurt, of course. That was the most important thing.

"I didn't mean for it to roll away." Matilda scampered out from under the table. "He was supposed to catch it." She pointed a little finger at the stranger accusingly.

Willow bit back her smile. She was supposed to instill good values in her daughter. Her job was to raise her into a responsible adult. It was just Willow now; she had to be both mother and father. But sometimes it was hard to stay strict when Tilda was so damn cute.

"Hey, take responsibility for your own actions," Willow reminded her daughter. "It isn't Mister..."

"Travis Kowalski, ma'am," the man provided helpfully. He widened his stance, drawing her glance down to his denim-clad thighs. This guy didn't skip leg day.

She nodded. "Mr. Kowalski isn't here to play with you. He's a customer." Putting on her best welcoming smile, she turned back to him. "And what can I help you with today? A jar of jam or preserves to take home, or one of our freshly-baked pastries?"

His sharp eyes scanned her store. She was proud of how she'd designed it, an eclectic mix of French provincial and American vintage. But there was a look in his eyes that told her he thought something was missing.

"Uh, do you have any pickles?" he asked.

"Pickles." She blinked. She tried to keep her voice even. Good service called for her to treat the customer as if he was always right. Even when he was a dumbass. "My shop is called *It's Your Jam*. Everything in here is jam, preserves, and occasionally a good jelly, or it has jam in it."

His lips twitched. "So, no pickles?"

"No pickles."

"You did that class on pickles," Tilda piped in. She scrunched her nose. "I didn't like 'em."

"That's only once a year. The rest of my classes are firmly jam-related." The phone in her apron pocket let out a sad chirp. She strode behind the counter. Her charger was already plugged in, and she pulled the charging end of the cord toward her and inserted it into her phone.

It fell out.

"You teach classes, Miz...?" He strolled to the counter opposite her and picked up a jar she'd stacked next to the cash register, hoping for last minute impulse buys. He brought with him the scent of something spicy, a nice contrast to the sweetness of her shop.

"Mrs. Janna." She grimaced. "Willow. I'm not much for formalities." She wiggled the charger. The little metal bit that went into her phone wiggled, too, loose. Her phone lit up, showing it was charging before going dark again.

His arm brushed hers as he reached for one of her cranberry apple compotes. "That's good to know." He cocked a hip against the counter and planted his hand next to hers. "There are some things I like to take my time with but formalities aren't one of them."

She blinked up at him, sweat beading at the small of her back. Did he mean those words to sound so suggestive?

He gave her a lazy smile as he leaned closer. Heat emanated from his body, making her nipples tingle.

Yes, he knew exactly what he was saying.

His gaze flicked down her body and his smile widened.

And he knew she was responding.

Flustered, she leaned back. She was not looking for hot men to flirt with. She was a single mother to a challenging eight-year-old and a business owner. She didn't have time for things like that. She didn't even remember how to flirt. Desperate to focus on anything except the gorgeous man in front of her, she turned toward her daughter. "Tilda, were you using my charger?"

"I tried to charge my tablet but it didn't fit." She picked at the toe of her shoe, peeling the sole an inch back from the canvas. Her red sock peeked through.

Great. New shoes and a new charger. She fiddled with her phone again. If she held the charger at just the right angle and kept pressure on it and her phone, a current flowed through. She jammed her phone up against the register, watched as the little battery icon lit up again, and blew out a breath. Maybe she just needed to buy shoes.

She swiped her finger across a speck of dust on the register. And now she had nothing left to fidget with and had to deal with the man who was inexplicably flirting. With her. "I'm sorry we don't have anything to interest you—"

"I definitely wouldn't say that." He arched an eyebrow.

"But I'm sure Barton's Country Store would have some pickles." She flicked her hand toward the door. "They'll be closing soon, so you'd better get going."

She hated directing people to that business. It wasn't a direct competitor to her because they sold a little bit of everything, but they did slap homemade looking labels on their crap commercial jams. With her quality ingredients and small batch size, she couldn't compete with their prices, a fact the owner knew very well. At the height of tourist season, he delighted in putting as many of his jams and jellies on sale as he could.

But damn the competition. It seemed more important getting this man out of her shop. Everything about him screamed *complication*, and she didn't need any more of those. She flapped her hand at the door again.

"Why, Miz Willow Janna, are you trying to shoo me away?" He widened his stance, apparently not wanting to be shooed.

She flushed. She opened her mouth. Closed it. She couldn't think of one thing to say. Any denial she made wouldn't ring true.

It was her daughter who saved her. "'Course not. That would be rude, and my mom is never rude."

Willow patted her updo. "Yes. Well—"

The bell above the door sounded, and Willow heaved a sigh of relief. "Welcome to *It's Your Jam*." She smiled at the group of three middle-aged women who'd entered. "Can I help you with something?"

A woman with graying hair stepped forward. "We heard you had…"

The lights went out. An eerie silence settled over the store. No hum of a refrigerator. No whirring from a mixer.

"Someone forgot to pay the power bill," one of the other ladies tittered.

Willow dropped her head. No matter how much she'd tried to fight it, she had to concede. Today was just one of those days where nothing went right. First a call from Tilda's school. Then a broken oven timer, causing her cherry anise tarts to burn. Followed by a fight with her newest employee.

"Excuse me, everyone. I'll be right back." Luckily there was enough light from the windows for the women to browse. Willow hurried into the kitchen. "Ben, did you use the microwave? You know it can't run the same time as the stand mixer."

Ben, a lanky twenty-something with greasy hair and a perpetual scowl, nudged a steaming mug behind him on the counter. "No."

She counted to ten in English, Then in French, the only words of that language she remembered from high school. Nope, she was still mad. "Go out front and see if you can make a sale. Please." She grabbed a flashlight from the drawer by the door to the alley and stomped outside. The sunlight seemed especially bright compared to the gloom of her shop.

Why was it so hard to find decent help? She'd lucked out when she'd hired Mandi before she'd opened, but when it had come time to find a second employee, it was like searching for a lode of gold with a chopstick.

She yanked open the breaker box and beamed the flashlight into the shadowy recess. That simile didn't even make sense. She was so frustrated, she was—

"Can I help?"

Willow jumped, spinning in mid-air. The flashlight flew from her hand. "Gah!"

Travis snatched the metal tube before it hit the ground. "Sorry. Didn't mean to scare you."

She pressed a hand to her heart. "No. I'm good. You just gave me a start. What are you doing out here?"

His eyes dropped to where her hand rested against her breasts then back up to her face. "I wanted to see if I could help."

She chuckled, but it sounded bitter. When was the last time she'd had help? When was the last time she'd trusted anyone to give her some? "It's fine. I just blew a fuse." She turned and toggled the switch for the north wall outlets, resetting it.

"That happen often?" he bent and peered into the box.

"Only when I run too many appliances at once."

He shut the box and turned. "You need to upgrade your electrical."

"I am aware." What she wasn't aware of was how she was going to pay for it. "I've discovered that running your own business means it's one problem after another. I'll get to this when I've put out a couple more important fires."

"You're running triage." He nodded, and handed her the flashlight. "I get that. It must be stressful."

She blew out a breath, a lock of hair floating back down to her cheek. "You have no idea." Somedays she wondered how she had ever thought opening up her own shop was a good idea.

"Which means you need someone to take you out and get your mind off of it." He opened the back door to her shop and guided her through, his palm on her lower back. "How about Friday night? I'll take you someplace you can have fun."

She paused. The hum of the refrigerator was the only reassuring thing in her life at the moment. "You're asking me out on a date? Just like that? We don't even know each other."

"That's usually how it works." The corner of his lips curled up. "Strangers go out together and get to know each other."

"Yes, but..." She swallowed. A date. She'd closed the door on that part of her life a long time ago. Travis was temptation on a stick, and she could hear her mom and sisters screaming at her to say yes, but that part of her life was over. At least until Tilda was grown. Lust and love and companionship had to take a backseat to raising her daughter, and finding ways to clothe and feed her.

Travis shifted, his tight tee stretching across his wide chest.

She bit the corner of her lip. Nope. No time for fun or dating or lust... Wait, she'd already listed lust.

She gave her head a little shake. "I'm sorry, but I don't date."

"Your daughter said you were a widow."

Willow nodded.

One of his pectoral muscles twitched. "So I wouldn't be stepping on any toes if I asked you out."

"That's one way to put it," she said, voice breathy. She needed to stop staring at his chest. But it was just so...broad.

Getting a grip on herself, she strode around him, heading for the front of the shop. Ben was handing a woman a bag. He even managed to thank her for her business.

"It's a good thing you got the power back on," the woman said. She angled her head at Ben. "I had to use my credit card. He couldn't make change from a twenty."

Willow nodded, her shoulders sagging. She'd assumed when she'd hired Ben that a high school degree and a couple of years at community college meant he had basic math skills. She'd assumed wrong. She needed to find someone else, but dreaded going through the whole hiring process again.

When the women had left, Ben whipped around. "It's not my fault you don't keep a calculator up here. And you told me you didn't want me using my phone while I was working."

"I didn't mean you couldn't use the calculator on your phone." She held up her hand and took deep breaths. "Please go finish the batter for the jam pockets. I'll be there in a minute to help."

He slunk around her. "Who uses cash anymore anyways?" he muttered.

"Mom," Tilda whined. "I want to get my new books. You said we could go to the bookstore this afternoon."

"That was before this day blew up." Willow rubbed her forehead. "I promise, tomorrow we'll go."

Tilda shoved her marbles into their cloth bag and slid her wrist in the end loops. "Sure we will." She made for the front door, her arms swinging. The marble bag caught the display of anise chokecherry jam.

The jar at the top of the pyramid wobbled, slid off its perch. Even Travis wasn't fast enough to catch it before it fell.

The glass shattered on the hardwood floor.

"Don't move." Willow used her deepest mom voice. Even Travis froze. She walked around the pastry counter and to her daughter. She swept her up and carried her away from any shards of glass before setting her back on her feet. "Go upstairs to your room. Start on your homework. I'll be up in a bit to help."

"Fine." Tilda hoofed it out of the shop. She yanked open the door immediately to the left of the shop that led up to their apartment and disappeared inside.

"Do you have a mop?" Travis asked. "I'll help you clean."

She went in the back and came back with a rag. One rag. She started scooping the mess into a small garbage can.

He crouched next to her. "I can—"

"I've got it." She smiled tightly. "Please make sure you don't cut yourself. It would be safer if you left."

"Safer for whom?" Amusement warmed his voice. It was like melted caramel over vanilla ice cream. "Are you nervous that I'm interested in you?"

She rubbed at a smudge of jam. "I'm perplexed, not nervous." And she was a liar. Everything about Travis made her edgy.

"What's confusing about it?" He cupped his hand around her elbow and helped her stand. "I saw you. I wanted to get to know you."

She gaped. "That's..." Creepy? Narcissistic? Weirdly sweet? "Direct."

His palm skimmed down her arm. "That's how I operate."

She believed him. Everything about Travis seemed straight-forward. Obvious even. From his strong, capable body to his interest in her.

Her life had felt unstable ever since her husband had died. She was forever casting about like a new sailor on a raging sea. The value of someone sincere, reliable, shouldn't be underrated.

But no matter how great a man Travis might be, it didn't change the facts. Her daughter was having trouble in school. Her business was barely in the black. Willow didn't have time to look for her own happiness. She didn't have time for Travis.

"I'm flattered." She pulled away from him. The moment his fingertips dragged from her skin, a chill settled in her body. "But no. I'm not interested in dating."

"A date with me isn't a task you'd have to take on," he said. "It's not a burden. It will be fun."

She took another step back, firming her resolve. "I said no. So unless you want to cross over into stalker territory, I think it's time for you to leave."

His gaze was piercing, seeming to see past her walls to the vulnerable woman within. But he dipped his head. "If that's what you want, I won't hound you anymore today." His lips quirked up. "But I will see you around. Have a good afternoon, Miz Willow Janna." He strode from the shop, taking all the energy in the room with him.

Willow dropped her head back on her shoulders. A man like him should come with a warning label. Extended exposure was hazardous to the health. Or at least to the nerves.

She plodded back behind the pastry counter and took out a blackberry mint jam pocket. She shoved half of the pastry into her mouth. If ever a day called for copious amounts of sugar, this was it.

She couldn't help but wonder if she'd let something even sweeter just walk out of her shop, however.

Chapter Three

Travis bore down against the leg plate, his muscles straining. The scar crossing his thigh went white against his tan skin. Sweat beaded on his forehead, but he pushed through the pain until his legs went straight.

"Should you be using that much weight?" Tony stood next to his machine, a white towel around his neck. The weight room on base was empty except for their squad. The usually soothing clank of metal hitting metal was more like nails on a chalkboard this afternoon.

"It's fine," Travis gritted out. As far as bullet wounds went, he'd been lucky. He could manage the pain. It was the fact he was benched that stung. He hated that he wasn't there for his squad. They'd already been out on one mission without him, and they'd been warned another one was imminent.

And they'd be leaving one man down.

"I can't believe your PT said"—Tony peered at the weights—"six hundred pounds would help with your healing."

Petty Officer Tony Garcia was the corpsman of their squad, and liked to take on a mother hen role. When Travis had been shot and bleeding out, Tony's medical knowledge had been welcome. Now it was just annoying.

"I said I'm fine." Travis rolled from the machine and swiped his bottle of water from the floor.

"Is it that time of the month for you, Skee?" Ryan Kelly, the communications specialist of their group, set down his kettle bell, smirking. "I hear warm compresses do wonders."

Travis inhaled sharply and cracked his neck. Would anyone really miss Alpha squad if he took them all out? Delta and Echo were almost as good as them. The security of the United States wouldn't suffer overmuch.

Chris strolled over, stretching. "He's just in a bad mood because instead of getting his dick wet in the hottie in Swansboro, he's had to rely on the ol' five-knuckle shuffle for relief."

He'd kill Chris first. No one would ever find the body. It didn't help his spiking anger that the man was partly right. All he'd thought about were Willow's curves, her plump mouth, as he'd jerked off in the shower that morning. His imagination was a poor substitute for the real thing.

"He couldn't even get her digits," Chris continued gleefully. "She turned One Shot down flat."

"How would you know, *Trip*?" Travis growled. "You weren't there."

Most of the guys in the military had a call sign. Chris hadn't earned his moniker until quite recently, and he wasn't so happy with what the guys had come up with. Travis was one of the rare men who actually had two nicknames. He'd been called Skee since bootcamp, a shortening of his last name, but quickly been tagged as One Shot once his sniper skills had shone themselves in the Raiders.

Chris gripped the top of the pull-up machine and stretched his back. "I read between the lines when you found me in the bike shop. Your evasiveness and pissy mood screamed that you'd gone down in flames." He pursed his lips. "Do you think his nickname applies to women? You know, he only gets one shot to get with them?"

Christ, wouldn't that be just his luck. The one woman who had just clicked for him, and it was over before it began. "This from the man who had to be pistol-whipped and hog-tied into his current relationship." Travis snatched his towel from the bench press seat and stalked toward the water cooler, careful to hide his limp.

Their squad leader, and fifth and final member of Alpha squad, Jake Skinner, stood in front of it. He held his ground, his eerie green eyes examining Travis before stepping aside. "You find yourself a girl?"

"Maybe." Travis filled his bottle. "She's...gun shy."

Jake nodded in understanding. His path to convincing his woman to take a chance on him had been rocky, to say the least. But now he, and somehow even Chris, found themselves in committed relationships. Travis saw how the women had settled his friends, brought a lightness to their eyes that the horrors of their job tried to extinguish.

Travis wanted that for himself. He wanted something deep, true. And now that he'd met Willow Janna, he knew who he wanted to try such a committed relationship with.

A cell phone buzzed, rattling atop the table they'd dropped their gear on. Another went off. Another. The men hurried to the table. Everyone had received a message.

Everyone except Travis.

"Wheels up in four." Jake grabbed his duffel. "Everyone take care of what you need to, and get back here ASAP."

Travis gripped the edge of the table. "I'm fully healed, Psych," he said, using Jake's call sign. "I can come."

Tony swung his own duffel, right into Travis's bad leg.

Travis winced, and tried to cover it with a scowl.

"Don't bullshit the medic on the team," Tony said. "You'll return to active when your body is ready. Until then, you'd be a liability."

The air was sucked from Travis's lungs. He wasn't a fucking liability. "I don't need a perfect leg to hold a sniper rifle."

"Yeah, it's just all the running and climbing to get into position that would be the problem." Ryan smacked his shoulder. "Don't worry, princess. You get to be a lady of leisure for the next few days. Enjoy it."

"Yep." Chris flicked his towel at him. "Until you learn to dodge enemy fire better, you're grounded."

His knuckles ached with how hard he was gripping the table. But if he let go now, one of his friends was going to have a black eye.

The men filed from the room. Jake turned at the door. "You do have time on your hands. Use it wisely."

Travis nodded.

Jake hefted his bag higher on his shoulder. "I found the Marines motto a useful mantra when it came to securing Caroline. Every time she threw up a wall, I'd adapt, improvise, and overcome." He grinned. "And now she's agreed to be my wife. See what progress you can make with your woman."

Travis straightened. He did have days ahead of him where nothing was required but some physical therapy and training. He could give almost his full attention to Willow. The edges of his lips curled.

"I'll tell Caroline she can call you if she needs something?" Jake asked.

"Of course." Travis sat back on the table after everyone had gone. What he needed was a plan. A way for Willow to get to know the charming, amusing, and fascinating man he was without her feeling like he forced his company on her.

He picked up his cell and did a web search. A smile stretched his lips.

This was going to be like shooting fish in a bucket.

Chapter Four

"I'VE SEEN A LOT in my thirty years in plumbing, but I've never seen this." The man Willow had called for her emergency toilet clog pulled his snake from the toilet bowl, a full baguette dripping from its end. "You have a kid?"

Willow dug her fingers into her hips. "Yes, but she wouldn't waste a good baguette like this." Willow had introduced her daughter early to the joys of a nice, crusty bread spread with a creamy camembert and maybe a chunky fig compote. If somehow Tilda had gotten her hands on a baguette, she wouldn't have shoved it down a toilet.

The plumber shrugged and dove back into the pipes. Each item he pulled from the clogged toilet he laid on a tarp on the bathroom floor. "Looks like a dozen jelly doughnuts. Lots of jam. And... lady, are these sticks of butter?" He blinked at her, accusing, like she'd wanted to flood the bathroom in her shop. There was only the one, and until this was cleared, her customers and employee were out of luck.

"I don't even sell jelly doughnuts." She barely kept herself from stamping her foot. That asshole. That contemptible, idiotic, absolute asshat of a—

"I think I've got it all." He flushed the toilet a couple of times. "But if that jelly had really hardened, you might have had to get new pipes."

Which was what she was sure he'd intended. Explode her costs of doing business until she had no choice but to sell.

"Thank you," she said stiffly. "Let my assistant know what I owe you, and she'll give you my credit card. But I have a class starting in five minutes that I have to get to."

She marched from the bathroom to the front of the shop. She almost wished she'd been wearing sneakers or boots, something that would allow her to really stomp her displeasure. But the delicate heel of her peep-toe, forest-green 1940s-style pumps wouldn't appreciate her temper. Her penchant for vintage-inspired shoes wasn't practical for working in a kitchen, but she loved them. And besides, they fit her brand.

"Is the toilet working again?" Mandi asked. Mid-twenties, her dirty-blond hair in a perpetual ponytail, her employee hopped off the stool behind the register and jerked her head toward the kitchen. "One of the attendees needs to use it, and by the way she's hopping around, she has Got. To. Go."

Willow nodded. "Five minutes. Is everyone set up in there?" Her weekly classes on everything from canning compotes to baking the perfect pavlova had become a hit. She could only fit eight students into her kitchen, but the additional income stream was steady and paid for her daughter's book habit.

"Yep." Mandi hiked up her slouching jeans. "A group of four friends, one couple, and one cutie."

Willow grabbed a full apron from the hook by the kitchen door. The skirt billowed out in a pinafore, and the bust was ruffled. She got so many comments on her aprons, she should really try to sell them. "Did you see Calhoun in the shop today?" she asked Mandi. "Or any of his henchmen?"

"Uh..." Mandi rubbed her chin. "I'm not sure I'd know what a henchman looks like. But his majesty, King Calhoun, didn't grace us with his presence."

The plumber strode from the back, carrying his toolbox.

Mandi glanced at him, and her eyes narrowed. "Do you think he had something to do with the clog?"

Willow lifted her shoulders. "It was intentional, petty, and childish."

"Yeah, that sounds about right." Mandi frowned.

"Intentional and messy. I put everything I pulled from it in the dumpster out back." The plumber held up a slip of paper. "Who's paying?"

She kept her gaze off the bill. She didn't want to see what the total came to. "Mandi, can you take care of that? You can go home after you pay him."

Willow headed into the kitchen, pasting a smile onto her face. A pair of amber eyes and a wicked smile made her pull up short. The door smacked into her hip, knocking her out of her shock.

Flushing, she greeted the class. "Good evening, everyone. I'm so glad you're here to learn how to make, and safely can, my strawberry daquiri preserves. If you haven't already, you can wash up at the sink there. Our ingredients are all on the tables. And the restroom is now open." She smiled at the woman who rushed past her and out the door.

Travis's eyes followed her, unrelenting, as she bustled around the kitchen. The skin at the base of her spine tingled, as though his gaze was a physical thing, something that stroked her in all the right places. She tried to ignore him, but it proved impossible. She snuck glances as she gave her standard jam spiel.

"Contrary to what we've always been told, we don't have to use a water bath when canning jams. As we cook up the strawberries, we let the jars heat up in the oven. We'll cook the preserves to a high enough temperature that when we pour it into the jars and seal them, it will sterilize the lids, too. This method only works with jams and preserves. Don't try it with your pickles. Now, every two people has a pot. Start mixing the ingredients. The recipes are on the table."

Travis unfolded from his stool. Even in her heels, he towered over her. It wasn't often she felt petite, but this man made her feel that way. "I don't have a partner," he said. "Will you join me?"

"Jam making doesn't need a partner." She smoothed her hand down her apron. Her heart thumped against her breastbone. She needed to get a grip. She'd been around good-looking men before. Never been pursued by one who looked quite as good as Travis, but still. She needed to get a handle on her hormones.

"A lot of things don't need partners." He gave her a lazy smile. "But they sure make things more fun."

Willow swallowed. "I need to teach everyone in the class, not just you."

"Ah, help a dude out." The other man in the class chuckled. "We can hear you just fine from there. I know I'm only here because I have a pretty lady at my side." He rubbed his date's back. "No offense," he said to Willow.

She pursed her lips. She felt like she should be offended, but her classes *were* very XX chromosome dominated.

Travis picked up the bowl of sliced strawberries and dumped them in a Dutch oven. "Where's your daughter? I thought she'd be here sticking her fingers in everything."

"Tilda doesn't stick her fingers in the food here." Most of the time. Willow measured out the lime juice. "And she's upstairs with her babysitter."

"You live upstairs?" he asked.

"Yep, I own the building, including the apartment above."

His arm brushed against her, and the hairs at the back of her neck rose. The faint scent of cedar and spice teased her nose, and her body swayed closer to the source.

"Impressive." Travis pulled the cap off a bottle of white rum.

"Not really." She stared at her hands. "I got an insurance payout when my husband died."

Travis blew out a breath. He reached out and covered her hand with one of his own. "I'm sorry."

His hand was warm, and much too comforting. She pulled away. "Why are you here, Travis?" she asked, voice low.

"I want to get to know you better."

She drew her eyebrows together. "You're paying for one of my classes to get to know me better?"

"Sure." He shrugged. "Men pay for dates to do the same thing."

"This is the modern age. Men don't have to pay for dates anymore."

He cocked a hip against the table and crossed one ankle over the other. "I do."

She didn't have a response for that. She fiddled with the ruffle on the bust of her apron, and Travis's eyes flicked down to her chest.

Which only made her more flustered. "I...I have to teach. Finish up your recipe." She pushed away from the table and walked among the other students. "Is everyone's preserves mixture ready to go? Okay, let's take the pots to the stoves."

She finished the class, trying to minimize her contact with Travis. Everyone was able to take home two jars of garnet-colored preserves. They chattered happily as they left the kitchen. Willow waited for Travis to exit. And waited.

"Class is over." She smiled tightly. "Thanks for coming."

He looked around at the pots and bowls littering the counters. "I'll help you clean."

God, that was sweet. "You don't have to."

He began gathering the dirty dishes and carried them to the sink. "I am very used to KP duty. It's no problem."

She sidled closer to him. The muscles in his forearms flexed as he moved. She was a sucker for a good set of forearms. "KP duty? You're military?"

He nodded.

"A Marine?" It was an easy guess with Camp LeJeune so close.

He nodded again. "I'm not afraid to get my hands dirty."

That statement seemed laden with innuendo.

Willow stalked to the sink. She didn't have time for innuendo. "I know you're probably used to women falling at your feet, but my mind hasn't changed. I have neither the time, nor the inclination, for dating." One of those, at least, was true.

"So you're going the nun route, huh?" His eyes twinkled.

"While the thought is appealing, I think they'd take away my shoes." She filled the sink with soapy water and started washing.

Travis grabbed a towel and took the first Dutch oven she cleaned. "And it would be a crime to hide that body under a habit," he agreed.

"Your sweet mouth isn't going to change my mind." She scrubbed at a bit of burnt strawberries.

He reached across her for the pot, his chest brushing her shoulder. "What will change your mind?" His husky voice sent shivers arrowing straight to her core.

She shoved a curl behind her ear. "Not that." She waved at his mouth. "And not all that." Her flapping hand encompassed his whole body. "I have a daughter who is flunking third grade and a business that is being sabotaged. Throwing a hot, sexy man into the mix will help nothing."

"Sabotaged?" He straightened. His shoulders seemed to expand, his muscles balloon. A smiling, easygoing Travis was panty-melting enough. An intent, lethal-looking Travis was scorching. "Tell me."

She licked her bottom lip. "Just a developer who wants to buy the property. It's nothing serious." Although if she'd had to replace her pipes, that would have been a serious dent on her bank account balance. But Travis looked ready to tear off heads. She wasn't willing to unleash him on Calhoun. "Silly pranks, really."

He studied her before slowly nodding. "If something more serious happens, you'll tell me."

Willow chose to hear that as a question. "No, I won't. This is my business and not your concern."

He opened his mouth to argue, but she cut him off. "I've been taking care of myself for a while now. I fight my own battles." She wiped her hands on her apron and strode for the table where his two jars of preserves waited. She pressed them into his hands. "I have to relieve my babysitter soon. Thanks for coming."

He seemed unconcerned with her dismissal. Travis tucked one jar in the crook of his elbow and opened the other.

"Wait! You're not supposed to open it yet. It hasn't sealed."

He shrugged. "I'll just stick it in the fridge." He dipped his pinkie into the mixture and put it to his tongue. A line creased his forehead. "Is it supposed to taste like this?"

She dipped her own finger in the preserves for a taste. "God no." She scraped her tongue against her teeth. It wasn't horrible, but when she knew how delicious the flavor should be, this was a horrible surprise. She sighed and leaned across the table, pulling a small bowl towards them. "You didn't add the sugar."

"I blame you." He screwed the jar closed. "You distracted me." One edge of his lip quirked up. "You have a bit of jam. Right there."

He cupped her jaw, and she held her breath. His thumb swept across her lower lip.

Their gazes locked.

Stepping close, he grasped a curl between his thumb and index finger. He dragged his fingers down, appearing fascinated as the curl stretched, then snapped back when he released it. He trailed his fingertips along her cheekbone, down her throat. "You are so fucking beautiful," he whispered.

She swallowed, her throat raw. She couldn't remember anyone ever looking at her this way, not even her husband. She didn't suffer from low self-esteem. She knew she was pretty enough, but she wasn't a great beauty.

But Travis made her feel that way. Travis saw her that way. And his penetrating gaze seemed to see beneath the skin, right down to her deepest, darkest desires.

He leaned down. His breath ghosted across her lips.

She remained absolutely still, not sure if she was more afraid of Travis kissing her...or leaving without one.

He pressed his mouth to her skin. It caught the edge of her lips, so far from where she wanted it she wondered if he meant to kiss her cheek. He sighed. "That right there is all the sweetness I need. I'll see you tomorrow."

He stepped back, saluted with his two ruined jars of preserves, and left.

She touched the spot he'd kissed. What had she just let happen? Why would she see him tomorrow?

And why was she so excited by the prospect?

Chapter Five

Travis rested his arm on the back of the bench. The front door to *It's Your Jam* was visible from his vantage point. The morning rush for pastries had died down, and now Willow was down to one customer per half hour roughly.

He smiled at a passing mother pushing a baby carriage. For the first time since his accident, he felt content. Useful. He was used to surveillance work. He was good at it. He'd finished his PT by nine, and had the entire day stretching endlessly ahead of him. He hadn't liked the sound of someone sabotaging Willow's shop, so keeping watch had seemed liked the easy call.

Plus, he was bored. He missed active duty. He knew the rest of his squad could take care of themselves, but he hated he wasn't there for them on this mission. Looking out for Willow was a pleasant distraction.

A silver Mercedes whipped into a parking spot across from Willow's shop. An older man wearing a white button-down and navy jacket hurtled out of the car, face red with fury. When he stomped across the street, Travis could see he wasn't wearing the bottom half of his suit. Instead, brightly checked golf pants clad his pudgy legs.

Travis rose as the man stormed into *It's Your Jam*. That definitely had trouble written all over it.

Raised voices coming from the shop had Travis quickening his step. He pulled open the front door and strode inside, his gaze scanning the room before settling on the man yelling at Willow at the front counter.

"I had a meeting at city hall to go to!" The man jabbed a finger at Willow. "When I told them I had to postpone because I had a mess on my pants, they thought, well, you can guess what they thought," he spluttered. "Because of you the mayor thinks I pooped my pants!"

Willow's lips twitched. Her face was a mix of amusement and horrified fascination. "If you had a set of golf clothes at your office to change into, why didn't you put on the golf shirt, too? So you wouldn't look like"—she flapped her hand up and down his body—"that."

Travis had been wondering about the clothing situation, too. And what Willow could have done to make a man ruin his pants. He had many questions.

The older man's face went even redder. "I didn't th— It doesn't matter." He jabbed his finger again, getting much too close to Willow's throat. "You should be ashamed of yourself. What kind of example are you setting for your daughter?"

Willow narrowed her eyes. "You're one to talk. You're lucky I didn't send you my plumbing bill."

Well, that answered one question. Travis stepped forward. "Is this guy harassing you?" He crossed his arms over his chest and stared down the other man. "Because if you are, it won't go well for you."

"This man is Mr. Beau Calhoun, and he was just leaving." Willow mimicked Travis's stance. She might have looked tough if it wasn't for her pin-striped, ruffly apron and puffed sleeves. With her red lips and dark curly hair tied with a ribbon, it was a look that hit him right in the groin.

Calhoun sneered. "I'm not scared of a little muscle. It's brains that ensure victory, and you, Mrs. Janna, had better start using yours."

Travis stepped closer, looming over the man, and drew his shoulders back. Brains were important, but brawn had its place.

Calhoun tugged on the lapels of his jacket. "Fine. I'll go, but this isn't over." He scanned the pastry display. "I'll have two raspberry tartlets to go."

Willow snorted. "Get out." She pointed at the door.

"Fine." The man sniffed. "I didn't want them anyway." He stamped out of the shop, looking as petulant as a little boy who'd been sent to time-out.

Travis watched to make sure Calhoun drove away. "The saboteur, I presume?"

A curl escaped Willow's low ponytail. She pushed it off her cheek with the back of her hand. "Unfortunately. Isn't there some saying that you can judge a person by the enemies they have? Well, my enemy is pathetic. I don't know what that says about me."

"You should have insulted him more." Willow's assistant, Mandi, if he remembered correctly, sidled out from the kitchen, looking at her phone. "I was hoping for more exciting footage."

"Footage? Were you filming us?" Willow asked.

"Of course." Mandi slid her phone into her back pocket. "If food had started flying, it would have gone on all the socials."

"Glad to know you have my back," Willow said sarcastically.

Mandi scratched her chin. "Well, if I had a GoPro or something, I guess I could have set up the camera then helped in a food fight."

Willow looked at her assistant, blinked, then turned toward Travis. "Can I help you with something?" She pasted her shop keeper smile on her face. "Since you don't like sweets, I fear you may be in the wrong store."

"I'm here to take you to lunch." She didn't need to know that he'd been watching her shop for over two hours. "I'm not too familiar with Swansboro so you'll have to choose the restaurant."

Willow smoothed her palm down the stomach of her apron. "I can't leave the shop."

"Sure you can." Mandi waved her hand at the empty room. "You know things won't pick up 'til the afternoon. I can handle it on my own."

"But..."

Travis could see the wheels spinning in her head, desperately searching for an out. He widened his stance. He didn't usually have to work so hard for a date. Women tended to throw themselves at him and his friends when they went out to bars. Something about the muscles and the military. The feeling of being the pursuer was novel. And stirring. He found he liked the chase.

As long as he was chasing the right woman.

Willow must have come up blank. She jutted out her bottom lip in an adorable little pout and started untying her apron. "Oh, all right. There's a Mexican place around the corner that has fast service."

She grabbed her purse and stepped out from the counter. Today she was wearing light purple pumps with little roses on the heels. They matched the flowers on her knee-length skirt and blouse.

His cock twitched. If and when he got this woman into his bed, her shoes would be making an appearance. Fucking her with nothing but her heels on was becoming his number one fantasy.

They walked the short distance. The scents of fruit and sugar rose from her skin, and Travis wanted nothing more than to lean down and lick a path up her neck.

Willow Janna would give him a sweet tooth if he wasn't careful.

"Thanks," she said, flustered, when he held out her chair.

He took the seat across from her. The restaurant was decorated in cheerful reds and greens, and large sombreros hung from the ceiling. The table they were at was made for two, and his long legs brushed hers as they sat.

"So, I have to ask," Travis said after the waiter left. "What did you do to ruin Calhoun's pants?"

Willow fiddled with her napkin. "I kind of put a couple of jelly doughnuts on his chair at his office." She peeked up at him, a faint blush staining her cheeks.

"Like a silent whoopie cushion." He shook his head.

"Hey, don't judge me. He put jelly doughnuts down my toilet, among other things." She pressed her lips together. "He deserved it."

Travis held up his hands. "I'm all for revenge." Behind Willow's adorable façade hid a devious, vindictive mind.

He liked it.

"Who is he?"

"Calhoun?" Willow twisted her mouth. "One of the largest property developers in the area. He's slowly been buying up the properties on my block. I think he wants to build high-end condos with commercial space on the bottom. But I like my location. It's Tilda's and my home. I'm not looking to sell."

"Why jam?" he asked.

A line creased her forehead. "In the doughnuts? Because that's what he stuck me with."

"No. Why create a whole business around jam?"

"Oh." She sat back, her face softening. "I spent summers with my grandmother. She taught me how to preserve food. My favorite was always the jams and jellies. Unlike you, I do like sweet."

"And so a business was born?"

She shrugged. "Food preservation is coming back in style. I just decided to narrow my focus to fruits."

The waiter brought them their drinks and they ordered. After he'd left, Travis leaned forward. "Something has been bothering me since last night."

She brought her hand to her mouth, her fingers caressing her lower lip. "Oh?"

"I don't want to be rude, but how does a kid fail third grade? She can't color in the lines?"

Willow's mouth dropped open. "That's what's been bothering you from last night? A comment I made about my daughter? Unbelievable."

He drew his eyebrows together. "What?"

She looked around them. They were isolated, but she still lowered her voice. "You kissed me! Sort of. I would think that would get a bit more of your attention."

He rested his hand over hers, trapping it to the table. "Feeling you beneath my lips doesn't bother me. Hot and bothered, yes. But that's not the same thing. But kissing you, sort of or otherwise, felt right."

"And I don't have time for kisses, sort of or otherwise," she retorted. "My schedule is full."

He stroked his thumb along her wrist. These little touches he had of her were torture. "I thought you'd go with 'jam-packed' there."

"I don't do puns." She sniffed.

He grinned. "Something else we'll have to work on." She opened her mouth, but he barreled on. "I'm surprised at you. You've devoted your life to giving people something sweet to enjoy, but you're denying yourself. There's all kinds of sweetness in life." He lowered his voice. "It would be a shame for you to miss out."

Her head flinched back. She stared at him, emotions swirling through her eyes. "I'll have to think about that," she said finally.

Travis nodded. It wasn't the full-throated endorsement of jumping into a relationship with him that he wanted, but then, he hadn't expected that. This was a mission with incremental successes. He'd slowly wear her down, and then do everything in his power to not let her regret her decision.

Their food arrived, and Willow seemed happy to focus on something else. She salted her enchiladas then dug in with gusto. "So tell me about yourself?" she asked. "What do you do in the Marines?"

He hesitated. His work in special forces wasn't something he broadcast. On the other hand, Willow wasn't going to be just a fling for him. "I'm a Raider. We're a division of SOCOM." At her blank look. "U.S. Special Operations Command."

Her fork paused. "Special forces? Like the Green Berets and SEALs?"

He nodded. "I don't have deployments like other members of the military. I could be here for weeks at a time, then be gone just as long. And when I get a call to go, I have to leave immediately. So if you can't get ahold of me all of a sudden, I'm not ghosting you." He smiled. "I promise."

She arched an eyebrow. "Who says I'm going to call you?"

"I do. In fact, give me your number."

She hesitated.

"I don't want it for phone sex, though we'll get to that, too." He winked, shifting forward. "I want you to call me if anything else happens to your business. Calhoun doesn't look dangerous, but I still want to know if he does anything further."

"I can take care of myself."

"And you do a wonderful job of it," he agreed. "Having backup never hurts."

She sucked her lower lip into her mouth. Finally, she nodded, and gave him her digits.

Travis texted her, waited to hear her phone beep. "Put me in your contacts. Call me if anything comes up."

She nodded again, her shoulders rounding.

"Hey." He took her hand and squeezed. "It's not a failure to get help. My buddies and I are all well-trained, but we still look out for each other."

"I suppose." She pulled her hand out from under his. "Tell me more about your work. Do you jump out of airplanes?"

"When it's called for." She was setting up boundaries again. He understood it, but didn't like it. Willow needed time to come around to the idea that she didn't have to carry the entire world on her shoulders. She had help now. "You ever jumped?"

"God, no." She shuddered. "I am not the adventurous type."

He tilted his head. "You opened your own business. You might be more adventurous then you think."

"There's no way I'm going skydiving." She pointed her finger at him. "Don't even think about that for date number two."

"So you admit this is date number one?" He chuckled at her frown. "Don't worry. I have no desire to see you fall from a plane." With the right preparation, skydiving was safe. But there were still things he didn't want to chance. Willow was one of them.

That didn't mean he didn't want to push her out of her comfort zone, however. He paid the bill and walked with her back to her shop. He could tell that a man like him was way out of her comfort zone. If he got her to try new things, maybe she could learn to accept him, too.

And he was more determined than ever to make that happen.

Chapter Six

THE SLAMMING DOOR RATTLED the jars of jam in the window display. Willow rested her elbows on the pastry counter and dropped her face into her hands. She loved cooking jam and baking. Loved the creativity of her recipes and even the design of her online storefront. But there were parts of being a business owner that just sucked.

And firing an employee was one of them, especially on a beautiful Saturday when the sun was shining in an idyllic blue sky. It just didn't seem right. But Ben had been rude to his last customer, at least a customer at her shop. Being understaffed was better than being badly staffed. And at least now there was one less employee to have to figure payroll taxes for.

"You can come out, Tilda," she called.

Her daughter slunk from the back hallway. "I didn't mean to eavesdrop. But when he started yelling, I decided to stay near the bathroom."

"I know, baby." Willow extended her arm. Her heart filled with warmth when her daughter nestled into her side for a squeeze. How much time did she have left of little girl hugs?

Of holding a tiny hand in her own? Tilda was growing up way too fast, and Willow was missing so much of it. "How about you help out your old mom, huh? I have a batch of anise star blackberry jam to make."

"Do I get paid?" Tilda squinted up at her, assessing.

She huffed out a laugh. "I can pay you in pastries. How's that?"

"Deal."

They made their way to the kitchen and Willow set her daughter up on a stool next to her work table. "Here's the recipe card. Read me the ingredients." As Tilda went through the list, Willow measured and poured until everything was in her copper jam pot. She hefted it to the stove and set the temperature.

She made two glasses of chocolate milk and set one in front of Tilda. "Your teacher called me."

Tilda's eyes went wide.

"You're not in trouble," Willow said. "She's worried that you're having a hard time in class. You're not finishing your assignments, she says." Which didn't make sense. Tilda was a good reader, and while not a whiz with math, she was able to work out the answers to the flash cards they went over.

Tilda wiped at her chocolate mustache. "The exercises are stupid. *A young cat is called a kitten. A young dog is called a puppy*," she intoned. "Why doesn't she let us read a good story and then ask us about that?"

"I don't know." Willow went to the stove and stirred the mixture. "But sometimes we have to do things even if they're not fun. I really didn't want to fire Ben today, but it needed to be done. You understand?"

"Yes, Mom."

Willow could virtually hear the eyeroll. She sighed. She didn't want to discourage Tilda from school by saying it was all drudgery. Learning could be fun. But there was a balance between enjoying school and completing her assignments, even the ones she didn't like.

Her phone vibrated on the worktable with an incoming text. "I can't stop stirring. Can you tell me what it says?"

Tilda stretched across the table and grabbed the phone. "Since you haven't called me back, I'm reduced to texting," she read. "How about tomorrow for date number two?" Tilda cocked her head. "Who's Travis?"

Shit. Willow turned off the burner. "Give me that." She held out her hand.

"Wait, is he the guy who caught you when you fell?" Tilda hopped off her stool and danced away behind the work table.

"When I slipped on your marble, yes."

The phone buzzed again. "Your website says you're closed Sundays when it isn't tourist season," Tilda read. She cocked her head and peered up at Willow. "Should I tell him you're closed Mondays, too?"

Willow darted around the table and snatched her phone from Tilda's hand. "No need to give him ideas." She texted back. *I can't. I don't have a babysitter who will come on such short notice.*

Hah. Sometimes being a single mom had its perks. A built-in excuse to get out of things she didn't want to go to was one of them. Her stomach sank. But she kind of did want to see Travis again. She bit her bottom lip, her heart doing a funny two-step at the thought of him. No. She drew her shoulders back. It was better to nip whatever this was in the bud.

Buzz. *No problem. I'll take you both out. I'd like to get to know Matilda better too.*

"Oh, come on," she muttered. Did he have to be so damn perfect? He was including Tilda in his wooing, and that just wasn't fair.

"He wants to see me, too?" Tilda leaned over her arm, peering at the phone. She bounced on her toes. "I haven't been to a movie for a long time. Or the zoo. Or maybe we can go on a boat—"

"Cool your jets." She rubbed her forehead. She hadn't taken Tilda anywhere fun for a while. There just wasn't time. And there still wasn't. Her schedule for tomorrow was already full with a shopping trip for fresh fruit at a local farmer's market, the monthly deep clean of the shop's kitchen, and setting up help wanted ads to replace Ben.

Tilda gripped her arm, looking up at Willow, her face so damn hopeful.

She ran her hand over her daughter's hair and gave in. "I'm not sure where Travis will take us, but we'll have fun no matter what." And before she could change her mind, she responded to say yes.

It could be good. If Travis wanted to take them somewhere age inappropriate for Tilda, Willow would steer him in another direction. He seemed easygoing. And afterwards, she'd tell him thanks, but she didn't have time to see him again. Easy peasy.

Her breath hitched. Even if she really wanted to see him again.

Chapter Seven

TRAVIS NEVER THOUGHT HEARING a woman shrieking in fright could be entertaining, but Willow was proving him wrong. It didn't help that Tilda had the most infectious little giggle he'd ever had the pleasure of hearing. Or that Willow was in absolutely zero danger, hovering as she was only four feet off the ground and flailing about like a drunken octopus.

His girl wasn't a thrill-seeker. Which made it all the more fun to push her limits.

"I wanna fly, too." Tilda bounced up and down, shaking her tiny tush in her one-piece flight suit.

Travis grinned. How had he not known that kids could be so entertaining? And useful. When Willow had balked at the indoor skydiving facility he'd taken them to, it had taken only one quivering bottom lip on her daughter to get her to agree to give it a shot.

"You're doing great," the instructor shouted to Willow. "How about a little more?"

"I guess?" Willow's face was pale underneath her helmet, but she gave her daughter a thumbs' up.

The instructor held one of Willow's arms, her leg, then leaned into the wind until he was airborne, as well. The two of them spiraled up the tube.

A string of curses filtered down to them, and Travis covered Tilda's ears. He was discovering all sorts of fun facts about Willow on this date. She swore like a sailor under high-stress situations. Well, high-stress for her. She tried not to discourage her daughter from exploring new things. And her ass looked fantastic in a flight suit.

The instructor might have been appreciating Willow's curves, too. Travis narrowed his eyes when the man's hand traveled too high up her thigh as he brought them both back down to earth.

Willow grabbed the edge of the door and pulled herself out of the flight chamber. Now that it was over, her cheeks and eyes glowed from the aftereffects of an adrenaline rush.

He went half-hard. Everything about this woman did it for him. Even her flattened hair when she took off her helmet looked sexy. He wanted to reach out and ruffle her curls.

And so he did.

She blinked up at him, looking surprised. But she didn't move away.

"Have a good time?" he asked.

"Okay, I'll admit it. That was fun. Well, it was fun after I became confident I wasn't going to fall on my face."

"My turn. My turn." Tilda plopped her helmet on her head. Her fingers fumbled over the chin strap.

Travis knelt and helped her secure it. "You remember everything you were taught?"

"Yep." She turned, ready to launch herself into the vertical wind tunnel.

Travis grabbed the back of her jumpsuit. "Whoa. Gotta wait for the instructor." He looked up to see the man leaning against the tunnel, his body angled toward Willow as he flirted and smirked and generally made an ass of himself.

Willow threw her head back and laughed at something he said.

Okay, maybe him being an ass was all in Travis's head.

He rose and glared at the instructor. "Tilda is ready to go."

"Great." The man squatted and held out his hand for a fist bump from Tilda. "Ready to fly?"

"Yeah!" She followed the instructor in, slowly leaned forward, and squealed as her feet left the ground.

Willow stepped close to him. She rested her fingers at the base of her throat. "Thank you for this. She loves it." She blinked rapidly.

He frowned. "Why do you look upset?"

She swiped at her cheek. "It's nothing. It's just moments like these that it hits me."

"What?"

She darted a look up at him. "How much her father missed. He would have loved to see her like this."

The muscles in his back tensed. This was new ground for him. He'd never pursued a woman who'd been married, and definitely not one who'd suffered such a loss. "Tell me about him?"

She blew out a breath. "He was a software engineer. We met in college and were together for a couple years before we married. He was...kind. Serious, but steady. Someone a woman could depend on, you know?"

Travis did know. He was glad that Willow had had that. And he couldn't deny he was a bit jealous. There were parts of her that would always belong to another man. "How did he die?"

"A brain aneurysm. One moment he was there, the next he was gone." She swallowed. "I don't think Tilda remembers much about him."

The girl in question screamed in delight as the instructor helped her flip end over end.

Willow placed her palm on the clear flight chamber wall, her eyes fixed on her daughter. "Sometimes I really miss him."

"I'm sorry." He couldn't think of anything else to say. He brushed his fingers across hers before gently intertwining them. He squeezed her hand, hoping to give her silent support. "Willow...?" He wanted to ask her so many things. Was she over her dead husband? Did she still love him? Was she willing to open her heart again? These were questions he needed the answers to, but knew they would be over the line.

"Yes?"

He cleared his throat. "Uh, I just like saying your name. Is it a family name?"

"No." Her lips twisted. "My mom just liked it. If they wanted to call me a flower, they should have gone with zinnia, or dahlia, something big and blousy. A slender willow reed really doesn't fit."

He turned to face her, tracing the curve of her cheek, the slope of her nose with his eyes. "I don't know what any of those flowers look like, but Willow is a beautiful name for a beautiful woman."

She froze. Their gazes locked. The noise of the flight center faded to a low hum. Travis leaned forward, caught in her gravity.

Tilda came charging out of the flight chamber, breaking the spell. "I want to do this every day, Mom." She threw her arms around Willow's waist before turning and giving Travis the same treatment. "Thank you."

His breath hitched in surprise. "Uh, you're welcome." He patted her back. He'd been disappointed when he'd realized he'd have to make this date a family one. He knew if he wanted to get close to Willow, Tilda came along as a package deal. But he'd hoped to get to know the woman better first, and some things couldn't be done with a child along.

But this...this was nice. Maybe family dates were the way to go.

Willow helped Tilda get out of her flight suit. "How about some pizza?"

Tilda threw her fist in the air. "Best. Day. Ever."

Willow rolled her eyes, smiling at her daughter. She looked up at Travis. "My treat, of course."

"No 'of course' about it. I asked you guys out. I'll get dinner."

They headed for the door. "But you paid for this," Willow protested. "I can—"

"This is an argument you won't win." Travis placed his palm on the small of her back as they exited. He scanned the parking lot before guiding them to his Jeep Commander. He lowered his head to whisper in her ear. "A date with me is full-service," he murmured. "Satisfaction guaranteed."

A blush started at her cheeks and swept down her throat. He peeked at the vee-neck of her shirt, wondering how far down the blush went. He'd told them to dress comfortably and casually, and seeing Willow in high-waisted jeans, a cream blouse, and old chucks made his mouth water.

She still looked classic, in a funky, unconventional way. And still looked sexy as hell.

His phone buzzed as he held open the doors for the girls. He pulled it out, a smile stretching his mouth as he read the message.

"Good news?" Willow asked after settling Tilda.

"My squad is back." All safe, thank fuck. He texted a response, then glanced sidelong at Willow. She seemed much more open to seeing him when the pressure of a one-on-one was gone. He needed more time with her, and his friends could help.

He settled behind the wheel and started the car. "The members of my squad are having a barbecue this week." They didn't know it yet, but they'd agree. "You and Matilda are invited."

"Oh, I don't—"

"Will there be hot dogs?" Tilda asked from the back seat.

"Of course. Wouldn't be a barbecue without them." He winked at her in the rearview mirror.

"Tilda has school." Willow rubbed her hand. "We can't go out on weekdays."

He reached over and stilled her nervous gesture. "We'll eat early. I'll get you back home in plenty of time."

"Come on, Mom," Tilda wheedled. "We have to eat."

Travis smothered a snort. He couldn't fault the kid's logic. And she was turning out to be an excellent wingman.

"Fine." Willow huffed, like eating good, grilled food was an imposition, but the edges of her lips curved up. She might act like she wanted to sit home each night, but he knew better.

What he didn't know was how available she was emotionally. Travis had engaged in many a battle, but he didn't know if he could fight a dead man for her heart.

Chapter Eight

Willow was in the middle of a batch of Rhuberry Delight when the power went out.

Mandi popped her head into the kitchen. "Uh, lights are off up front."

"Everything's off." She moved her pot of jam, scowling. She should have upgraded her stove to gas-powered, but when she'd bought the building, the expense of adding gas had curdled her stomach. Now, she couldn't cook. "And I wasn't even using the mixer," she muttered.

She stomped outside to the breaker box. The door wasn't closed all the way, and she frowned. Yanking it open, she examined the switches.

There were all aligned in perfectly straight rows. Rats. There went her easy fix. Just to be sure, she pushed all the switches to the off position, then back to on. She made sure the door was fully latched before returning inside.

The fridge was still silent. The lights still off.

Willow dropped her head back onto her shoulders. After all this time of playing footsie with the fuse box, she was going to have to call an electrician.

Who couldn't come out until tonight.

She ended the call and stalked to the front. "We're closing early," she told Mandi. "Unless the power miraculously just comes back on, we're down for the count."

"Did you pay the utility bill?" Mandi asked.

"Of course, I paid the bill." Willow took her apron off and hung it on the hook. Though calling the power company wasn't a bad idea.

Except they had no answers for her, either. She tossed her phone onto the counter. "Okay, now it's official." She went to the front door and turned the sign from open to closed. "Take the rest of the day off. Oh, and take whatever pastries you can eat."

"Are you sure you want to close?" Mandi took a muffin filled with huckleberry jam and slid it into a bag. "Unlike some, I can make change if people want to pay cash."

"Not enough people pay with cash anymore to make it worth our time." She pointed at the pastry display. "And take more than that. They'll be stale by tomorrow."

Mandi filled a couple more bags. "Okay. See you tomorrow?"

She slumped onto the stool by the register. "I'll let you know."

After her employee left, Willow dropped her head to the counter to rest on her arms. It wasn't a big deal, she told herself. She'd get her electricity fixed and be back in business.

But why did everything have to be a hurdle? Why couldn't her business just run smoothly for once?

The backs of her eyes burned. Why was everything just so hard?

And speaking of hard, she was going to have to tell Tilda they couldn't go to the barbecue tonight. And she'd have to tell Travis. She didn't know which she dreaded more.

She blew out a breath. She did know sitting here feeling sorry for herself wasn't helping anyone. She pulled herself upright and picked up her phone.

"Hey there." Travis's voice rolled over her, smooth as honey. "I didn't think I'd hear from you 'til later."

She scratched at a mark on the counter, her arm feeling heavy, sluggish. "Hi, Travis. I'm sorry, but I can't come tonight."

"Why?" His tone lost its lazy drawl, became focused. "Is something wrong?"

Willow wanted to laugh. Or scream. Something was always wrong. "Nothing big. My power's out again, and this time it's not a flipped switch. I have to wait for the electrician, and since he's squeezing me in at the end of his day, it might be late."

Sounds of a muffled conversation came over the line. Then Travis was back. "I'll be there in two hours. See if we can get your problem figured out."

"You know electrical work?" She tugged on her lower lip. "Uh, no offense, but I really want someone who's trained to work on my building."

He chuckled. "I have a buddy who flips houses and does all the electrical upgrades himself. Don't worry. He knows what he's doing."

"Oh, okay." Her pulse beat faster. She was going to see Travis today after all. Which didn't matter to her, of course. She was still set on keeping things...friendly between them and nothing more. But maybe he'd still be in the shop when Tilda got back from school. Her daughter couldn't stop talking about the man who'd taken her 'flying.' Willow was glad Tilda would get to see her hero of the day.

She cleared her throat. "Well, I'll be here. I'll see you when I see you."

"Two hours," he repeated then hung up.

Two hours. She resisted the urge to run upstairs and redo her hair and makeup. It didn't matter what she looked like to Travis. In fact, maybe the more rumpled and greasy she looked the better. If he lost interest, stopped pressing her, then maybe...well, maybe she'd have a chance to resist.

Two hours with no power, no internet. She couldn't cook or update her website or do any of the hundreds of other tasks she needed to.

But she could catch up on her deep-cleaning.

She grimaced and headed to her closet for supplies.

Travis arrived almost exactly two hours later, with a black-haired, green-eyed Adonis at his side.

"You're not an electrician," Willow stated. Electricians didn't look like Greek gods, and this guy just needed a toga to be Apollo come down from Mt. Olympus. His muscles were on par with Travis's, and he had the same confident stance. "You're a Marine."

"Guilty as charged." He flashed her a toothy grin.

Travis stepped forward, looking sinful in faded jeans and a tight white T-shirt, and brushed a kiss across her cheek. He did it casually, as if he'd been kissing her his whole life.

Willow tensed, not sure if it was because she didn't like his presumption, or because she liked it too much.

"This is Chris Gunn, one of my squad mates," Travis said.

Chris shook her hand. "I do know what I'm doing. I worked with my dad, a contractor, for years, and I always get a clean pass from inspectors when I do my own work."

And the price was right. If Travis's friend could fix the problem, she could call off the costly repair man. "All right. Thanks for coming out. All the power just went off but it doesn't look like any fuse is blown."

"The box is out back?" he asked.

Willow nodded as the bell above her front door rang again. Two women in their mid- to late-twenties stumbled inside, their gazes darting all over the shop before landing on her.

"I'm sorry, but I'm closed," Willow said.

"Like that would stop them," Chris muttered, shaking his head fondly.

"We're not here to shop," a pretty woman with pale blond hair said, "although it smells delicious. I don't know how I've never been here before."

The other woman, a brunette with an athletic build, strode forward. "I'm Sam and this is Caroline." She jerked her chin at her friend. "We're with Travis's friends in the squad. That one's mine." She pointed at Chris, who waggled his eyebrows. "We wanted to meet the new girl."

Willow looked to Travis, then back at the women. What had he told them about her? "Um, I wouldn't exactly say I'm the—"

Caroline elbowed Sam. "You know he hasn't landed her yet. He's still trying to reel her in. Don't scare her off."

"Oh, good lord." Travis looked skyward. "You told Sam where we were going?" he asked Chris.

The man shrugged. "I had to tell her I couldn't shop for the meat with her this afternoon. She wanted to know where I was going instead."

Travis planted his hands on his hips. "Willow, I'm sorry. I—"

"Oh, don't apologize for us. She was going to meet us tonight anyway." Sam made shooing motions. "Go fix the power while we get to know her. I promise not to reveal *too* many embarrassing secrets about you." She grinned.

Travis grumbled as he led Chris into the kitchen. The door swung shut behind them.

"We really aren't here to hassle you," Caroline said. She lifted a shoulder. "We just haven't seen Travis so interested in anyone before. We were curious."

Sam pulled out a chair at one of the tables and plopped down. "Plus, if we're here, we can't be responsible for barbecue prep. It's a win-win."

Willow couldn't fault their logic. Or their curiosity. She didn't mind the opportunity to quiz Travis's friends, either. "Do you want a soda or water?" She moved to the small refrigerator behind the counter. "They should still be cold enough."

"That would be great." Caroline bent until her nose was nearly pressed against the pastry display. "Any chance we could try one of these, too?"

"God, yes." Willow pulled out plates and napkins. "In fact, you guys should take them all to the barbecue. I'm not selling them today and I hate to throw them out."

Sam came over to pick out a treat. "You don't have to twist my arm."

"You could give them to a shelter, maybe." Caroline said.

Willow snorted. "The regulations about giving away food are a minefield. Restaurants have been busted for giving meals away to the homeless."

"Bureaucracy," Sam muttered. "I work for the city of Jacksonville, so I know what you're talking about."

They settled around the table. "So tell us about yourself," Caroline said. "We want to know everything."

Willow spread her hands. "What you see is what you get. I'm a single-mom jam-maker, just trying to save enough for a college fund for my girl."

Sam took a bite from her jam pocket and moaned. "And an amazing baker. If Travis doesn't snap you up, I will."

Caroline arched an eyebrow.

"What?" Sam took another bite. "I could go both ways if it meant steady access to these pastries."

Caroline took a bite of a blackberry thumbprint cookie. Her eyes flared wide. "I see what you mean." She finished it off and reached for another. "Tell us about your daughter."

That was easy. Willow launched into all the reasons Tilda was the best daughter ever. She had to cut herself off at some point. Rationally she knew no one else but her would care about the time Tilda brought home a wild baby bunny, but the urge to describe her kid in minute, loving detail was great.

"She sounds like a doll," Sam said.

"She'll be home from school soon." Willow looked at the clock. "You'll probably get to meet her."

"If not now, then at the barbecue tonight." Caroline dabbed her lips with a napkin.

"If the electrical gets fixed." Willow sagged back in her chair.

"Chris will fix it," Sam said confidently. "He'd better, after the trouble Travis went through to set up the barbecue."

Willow drew her eyebrows together. "What do you mean? I thought his friends were having the barbecue."

Caroline smacked Sam's shoulder.

"Oops." Sam shrugged. "It doesn't hurt for her to know what she's getting into."

Caroline thought for a moment, then nodded.

"What am I getting into?" What exactly were they serving at this barbecue?

"Travis told you about his job, right?" Caroline asked.

Willow nodded.

"Well, we've had to learn the hard way that Raiders, well, probably every special forces guy, are extremely determined." Caroline turned in her chair to face Willow.

"Pig-headed, really," Sam added.

"And when they set their sights on something, or someone, they give it their all." Caroline's eyes lost focus, a small smile dancing across her lips. "It's sweet, really."

Sam rolled her eyes. "What she's trying to say is that Travis wants you. So he's going to do everything in his power to get you. Including telling Tony that he's having a barbecue at his house, and an early one at that because your daughter has school tomorrow."

"Ah." Willow straightened her legs and crossed her arms over her middle. Travis was smart. He'd tailored each of their "dates" to suit a single mother. But did that make him devious or thoughtful? It probably depended on what he wanted. Was he in it for a quick lay, or did he want an actual relationship?

And what did she want? She'd thought she'd known, but now she wasn't so sure.

"Travis really is a good guy," Sam said. "And I'm not just blowing smoke up your seriously adorable skirt."

Caroline's gaze flicked down to Willow's black ruffled shirt and skirt, dotted with tiny pink hearts. "Yeah, we're going to have to go shopping together."

"That's definitely happening," Sam agreed. "But on a more serious note, I hope you give Travis a chance. These guys make time spent with them worth your while."

"I...I'll have to think about it. But I'm just so busy." That reason had seemed so solid just hours ago. Now it sounded like a weak excuse from someone too timid to live.

The kitchen door swung open, and Travis and Chris came through, their faces grim.

Willow's shoulders dropped. "It can't be fixed. I'm going to have to sell this place at a loss and move, right?"

Travis's lips edged up. "It can be fixed."

"I just need to get a few parts and I'll have you back up and running in a half hour," Chris added.

"Then what's the problem?" Their faces did not scream easy repair.

"I removed the breaker box to look at the wiring behind it." Chris ran his hand up the back of his head. "Sure enough, several wires were damaged. One of them probably caused a power surge that blew your system."

"Okay," Willow said slowly. "What caused the damage?"

Chris and Travis looked at each other.

"It could be squirrels or rats," Chris said. "They're typically the culprits in situations like these.

Willow's back tingled. She didn't like the idea of rats so close to her kitchen. But from the sound of Chris's voice, vermin was probably the best answer.

"It didn't look like teeth marks on the wire casings." Chris frowned.

Travis strode up to her and squatted by her chair. He rested a hand on her knee. "It looked like tool marks. I think someone tampered with your electrical."

Chapter Nine

TRAVIS STRODE DOWN THE locker room's hallway, his hair still damp from his shower. Even after his strenuous PT and evaluation, his leg barely twinged. He hardly had to work to hide his limp.

"You clocking out already, Skee?" Ryan and the rest of the guys piled through the door on Travis's left, each wearing their camo BDUs and carrying rucksacks. They'd come from underwater demolitions training, something Travis was irritated he'd missed. "Remind me to get shot next mission," Ryan said. "Fast way to easy street."

Travis changed direction and met his friends. "Fuck off," he said good-naturedly. "Besides, my days of leisure are near an end. I just got cleared for active duty, starting Monday."

Tony slapped him on the back. "Oorah."

"Welcome back," Jake said. "How about a round at *The Limber Ginger* to celebrate?"

"I—"

Tony cut Travis off. "Hey, let's try that new bar on Sycamore, instead. I've been wanting to see what the hype is about."

"But I—" Travis began again.

"All the bars on Sycamore are infested with hipsters and office-dwellers." Chris snorted. "That's a negative, ghostrider."

Ryan smacked Tony on the shoulder, making the man stumble. "We know you like your woman all sophisticated and professional and shit, but the rest of us prefer someone more down to earth. We're going to the *Ginger*."

Tony flexed his wide shoulders. "The only down you like when it comes to women—"

"I can't go," Travis all but shouted. Christ, but his friends could be annoying. Had he really been eager to rejoin this squad of men? *Yes.*

Four sets of eyes peered owlishly at him, and he lowered his voice. "I already have plans."

Jake arched an eyebrow. "Where you heading to?"

Travis clenched then flexed his hand. It was true he couldn't wait to be back with his team, but injured duty had provided one benefit. Time to spend with, and look out for, Willow. Time he now needed to use wisely.

"I have a visit to pay over an electrical problem." Chris had been able to replace the damaged wires in Willow's building and gotten her back up and running. But all through the barbecue last night, Travis could see she had been worried. Her smile hadn't been as bright. Her shoulders were a bit too tense.

And she was right to be uneasy. Sabotaging her electrical could have led to much more than a power outage. Calhoun could have caused a fire. A fire with Willow and Tilda inside the building.

Travis ground his teeth. If it was Calhoun. He needed to find out, and put the fear of God into the man if it was.

"This property developer you told us about last night?" Tony asked.

He nodded. Travis had done some research. Willow's shop was considered downtown, but it was a section that petered out into an industrial-commercial mix. When she'd purchased the building, the price had been moderate as it was a couple blocks out of the tourist section.

With its proximity to the water, however, a redeveloper could turn the area into something upscale.

Jake stared at him, his gaze intent. "Want company?" he finally asked.

Travis inhaled sharply. "Don't trust me not to lay hands on a civilian?"

Jake dipped his chin and raised an eyebrow. "Sometimes even civilians need to be taught a lesson. I just thought having a couple more of us with you could be...effective."

Travis's shoulders slid down his back. He didn't know why her was so touchy. Being down for a couple months had made him disconnected from his squad. He'd been feeling useless, but that didn't mean they thought he was.

"Yeah." Travis rubbed the back of his neck. "A show of force always helps." Calhoun had said he wasn't afraid of muscle, but with five Raiders showing up on his doorstep, that made even the bravest of men tremble.

Travis didn't peg Calhoun as the bravest of men.

"Give us ten." Jake nodded to the rest of the guys and they strode for the locker room.

Nine minutes later, they were ready to go. They took two vehicles to Swansboro, parking in the business section of town. Travis's lips twitched as they strode for the building Calhoun's office was located in. All his friends wore shirts that showcased their muscles, boots, aviator glasses, and ice-cold expressions.

Yeah, Calhoun would fucking feel fear.

In the stairwell to the second floor, Travis said, "Calhoun is a small, older man. This truly does have to be hands-off." Though if Calhoun's actions had hurt Willow or Tilda, the man's age and size wouldn't have stopped Travis.

"Don't worry." Chris shot him a shark's grin. "Operation Make-Him-Shit-His-Pants will be completely psychological."

Ryan groaned. "Can't we make it Operation Piss-His-Pants? I don't want to deal with old man poop."

"Jesus," Tony muttered. "I can't believe I risk my life for you people."

Travis pushed open the door, and his friends fell silent. Calhoun's offices took up the entire second floor. The receptionist's desk was off to the right in front of the elevator. He hung a left. He didn't need Calhoun having advance notice of their visit.

And because he and his squad walked with purpose, no one challenged them or asked their business. Travis read the nameplates at each door before stopping at Calhoun's office. The door was half open, and Travis pushed inside.

Calhoun's eyes widened. He fumbled with his mouse, closing a program on his computer, but not before Travis could see what he'd been doing. Christ, the man was playing Mahjong. It was like the universe was sending him another message, underlined in red. Elderly man. Do not punch.

His friends spread out, flanking the desk. They hadn't removed their shades and stood grim-faced, arms crossed over their chests.

Calhoun ran his fingers over his balding pate. "What do you want?"

Travis had to hand it to him. The man's voice hardly quavered.

"You remember me?" Travis pushed his sunglasses to the top of his head. "From *It's Your Jam*?"

Calhoun frowned. "Mrs. Janna's friend. I remember you. I don't see why you're here, though. We don't have business together."

Travis stepped close so he could rest his palms on the desk. He lowered his head so they were almost eye to eye. "I want to be clear. Ms. Janna's property is not on the market. She will not be bullied into selling. Any further attempts to sabotage her building will be retaliated against with extreme prejudice."

The older man sniffed. "I don't know what you're talking about. She can't prove I had anything to do with her plumbing problems. Besides"—his eyes flashed with outrage—"she already got even with me for that."

Travis's eyes flicked to the executive chair Calhoun sat on. It must have been the location of the jelly doughnut incident. He bit the inside of his cheek. Willow was a firecracker, no doubt about it.

His amusement faded. This wasn't fun and games anymore. Calhoun had upped the ante.

"A mess on your pants doesn't compare with trying to wreck the plumbing in her building." Travis made his voice go low and mean. "And it certainly doesn't compare to taking out her electrical system. You could have caused a fire." He spun the man's chair so he faced him, then gripped the armrests. "You got lucky. If you'd started a fire, putting Willow and her daughter at risk, well, we'd be having a much different conversation right now."

Calhoun gaped at him like a guppy. "Fire? I didn't...I wouldn't...I don't know what you're talking about. And if you continue to harass me in this manner, I'll call the police."

Travis locked his gaze on the man's faded blue eyes, trying to read what lay beneath. There was a hint of fear there, but being surrounded by five predators was enough to make anyone feel like prey. There was also anger. Surprise.

Surprise at being caught? Or did he truly not know about the tampering?

Travis growled deep in his chest. "Tell the cops to look up the report Ms. Janna filed yesterday. Then they'll know what I'm harassing you about, at least." He pushed up and spun Calhoun back to his desk. "If anything further happens to *It's Your Jam*, you'll be seeing me again."

He slid his sunglasses down to cover his eyes. "You don't want to see me again."

He filed out, his friends following. When they hit the sidewalk, Travis stopped and drew in a drag of fresh air.

"He's got balls of steel for an old dude." Ryan scowled. "I wanted more quivering. Some tears. At least a bit of begging."

Jake looked up at the sky before shaking his head. "Did you believe him?" he asked Travis.

"I don't know." And that pissed him off. He was usually good at reading people. In his job, he had to be. "He's an entitled prick who thinks he deserves Willow's building. He definitely fucked with her pipes. But the electrical?" He shrugged.

Jake nodded. "Let us know if you need any more help." He jerked his chin at the guys. "Come on. Let's get back to base. You coming with?" he asked Travis.

He shook his head. He was in Swansboro. He wasn't going to pass up the opportunity to see Willow.

"Going to her shop?" Tony asked.

"Yeah." Travis stretched his back. Seeing his little bit of sweetness would get rid of the sour taste Calhoun had left in his mouth.

"Don't you think you're laying it on a little strong?" Tony rubbed his jaw. "You just saw her last night."

"Pussy-whipped is what he is." Ryan's voice dripped with dispair. "What the hell is going on with our squad? All the single men are falling."

Everyone ignored him.

Travis lifted a shoulder. "I want to see her. A couple times a week isn't enough."

Jake and Chris nodded in understanding. "Get me some more of those home-made poptart things," Chris said. "Maddie loved them."

Tony snorted as they moved toward their cars. "Sure, blame your sugar fix on your girlfriend's little sister."

"Asshole, she did like them," Chris insisted.

Travis got in his Jeep and waved goodbye. He loved his friends. Since Travis only had two sisters, they truly were the brothers he'd never had. But, damn, they could drive even a Morman to drink.

Luckily, he was heading to the one person who made him feel centered. Whole. He knew Willow wasn't there with him. Not yet. But Travis had no illusions about himself.

He was getting in deep. And he couldn't bring himself to think that was anything other than wonderful.

Chapter Ten

TRAVIS LOOKED ABSURD SITTING hunched over her kitchen table helping Tilda with her puzzle. He dwarfed the rickety chair. He looked like Alice after eating the cake.

Or was it after she drank that she grew?

Willow dried the last plate and put it away. Having Travis over for dinner at her small apartment above the shop had been weird. He seemed so out of place in her home, but then, any man would. She'd never invited one up before.

She leaned back against the counter and took a sip of her wine, watching him with her daughter. She had to admit, having him here also felt...nice. Weirdly nice? Was that a thing? He brought a different energy which she couldn't help but respond to.

Tilda gave a little fist pump as she pressed the last piece into place.

One side of Willow's lips curved up. She should probably be worried about Tilda becoming too attached to the man. After all, he'd just appeared out of nowhere one day. Even though he'd managed to thread his way into their lives, making it hard to remember a time she hadn't known him, he could disappear just as quickly.

She felt too content to worry. She'd pull a Scarlett O'Hara and think about it tomorrow.

"Bedtime," she said. Tilda had already washed up and donned her PJs after dinner. All that was left was story time. They'd been reading a chapter a night from *Harry Potter*, but if they continued that tonight, she'd have to kick Travis out first. Something she wasn't eager to do.

Tilda made it easy on her. "Just a little later, Mom? Can't we watch TV?"

"One program." Willow bet Tilda wouldn't last ten minutes. "Go choose one."

Her daughter ran into the living room.

"Do you want another glass of wine?" she asked Travis. Her heart made a strange flopping motion. She should want him to decline, to take his leave.

She didn't want him to go.

"Better make it half a glass." Travis stood and stretched. "Thanks for dinner again. When I showed up on your doorstep, I thought I'd just be saying hello. I didn't think I'd be lucky enough to spend the rest of the day with you and Tilda."

Willow poured more wine. "What were you doing in Swansboro? More shopping?" she teased.

"God no." They wandered into the living room and settled on the sofa. Tilda was lying on the floor in front of the TV, a cartoon playing. Her head was already nodding.

"I came to have a word with Calhoun," he said in a low voice.

She tucked her legs up beneath her. She still wore her dress, but she'd kicked off her heels the moment she'd stepped inside her apartment. "Why? Are you looking to invest in real estate?"

He dropped his chin and gave her a look.

Her cheeks heated. Okay, so if he wasn't talking to Calhoun about business, that could only mean....

"You talked to him about me?" she squeaked.

"Of course." He rested his arm along the back of the sofa, his fingertips grazing her shoulder. "He has to know there are consequences to his actions."

She blinked. She'd heard about men who liked to help women out, be their champions, but she'd always thought of them like unicorns. A pretty dream with no basis in reality. "I don't know whether to be furious that you interfered in my business or grateful that you cared enough to do so."

He gave her an impish smile. "I pick grateful."

She slapped his arm playfully. He wore a lightweight blue Henley today, and she let her fingers linger on the bulge of his biceps. "I don't think you get a choice in how I feel."

His face sobered. "I hope that's not the case. I'm trying very hard to make you happy."

Her breath hitched in her throat. She didn't know how to respond. She was so out of practice when it came to this. She and her husband, Bill, had been friends first. The transition to lovers had been effortless. Uncomplicated.

Everything about Travis screamed complication. Just being with him was a challenge. A challenge to control her emotions. Her actions.

Her heart.

"Tilda's out." He nodded his head toward her unconscious daughter.

"I'll, uh, put her to bed." She started to rise, but Travis put his hand on her shoulder.

"Let me get her," he said. "She already gave me a tour of her bedroom." The corners of his eyes crinkled. "I know where it is."

Willow merely nodded.

Travis gently scooped Tilda up, cradling her to his chest, and Willow's heart clutched. Seeing him holding her sleeping daughter as though he held something fragile, precious, did things to Willow on a primal level. Her ovaries screamed at her to start making more babies with this man. Her body softened, wanting to let him in. Even her mind was coming around to the idea of allowing him into her life.

Travis came back into the living room, empty-handed. "She is safely snoring under her rainbow comforter," he reported. He dropped back on the sofa. "She really is a great kid."

Unbidden, panic clogged her throat. She snatched his wrist, holding it tight. "Please. Don't be like this if you don't mean it."

He frowned. "Be like what?"

"Caring. Charming. You say all the right things to make me and Tilda...." She swallowed. "Don't say it if you don't mean it.

I could take it if you did all this then walked away, but I couldn't take it if Tilda got hurt." And her girl would get attached. Come to expect that Travis would be there for her. That he'd be someone she could depend on. She'd be devastated if this was just a game to him. If *they* were just a game to him.

Travis turned his wrist and took her hand. He gazed at her steadily. "I don't say what I don't mean. I can't promise you I'll never fuck up, but I can promise that what you hear from me is true."

She looked at their entangled fingers, his hand so much bigger, stronger than her own. "You scare me," she whispered.

He swept his thumb over her wrist. "How?"

"My life can be hard," she said, shaking her head, "but it's safe. Predictable. Some people might find that boring, but there's comfort in it for me."

"You scare me, too."

Willow huffed out a laugh. "I highly doubt that."

He placed a finger under her chin and raised her head. "You're so much more than any woman I've been with before. The stakes are so much higher with you because I'm not just looking for a good time. I'm scared I'll let you down. Let Tilda down. And I couldn't live with myself if I did. But love is worth the risk."

She ran a hand through her hair. "Love? I'm not sure I know what that is, at least not in the romantic sense."

"But you were married." A line creased his forehead.

"I did love my husband." She scraped her teeth over her bottom lip. "But when we were dating, it was never some great love affair. And when we got pregnant, we decided it was best for the baby to get married. I don't regret that decision, and I don't think Bill did, either, but he never made me feel...."

Off balance. Like she was at the top of a roller coaster about to take the plunge. The feeling Travis gave her bordered on exhilarating and nausea.

"Let me ask you this." He edged forward until their knees met. "In twenty years, what will you tell Tilda. To play it safe, stay alone? Or to take a chance on having everything?"

Jeez, when he put it like that. Of course, she'd want Tilda to have wild, passionate love. She wanted her to experience everything life had to offer.

And maybe she should want that for herself, too.

Slowly, tentatively, she leaned forward. Travis didn't move, making her travel the full distance to him. She paused when they were inches apart. His breath ghosted across her lips. His scent, an intoxicating mixture of cedar and spice, clouded her mind.

Praying she wasn't making a mistake, she pressed forward that last inch and kissed him.

Chapter Eleven

His lips were warm, responsive, but Travis let her do the exploring. His hand remained still within hers. His mouth accepted her invasion, joining in the slip and glide of her tongue but going no further. He was definitely letting her take the lead.

Until he wasn't.

With a growl, he wrapped his arm around her back and tugged her close. He leaned back so she was laying on top of him, never letting their kiss break. He fisted his other hand in her hair as he turned the kiss hard. Devouring. Like he needed to hold tight to her or she might slip away. The ache in her scalp made her tremble.

No one had ever wanted her this much.

She'd never wanted anyone this much.

He angled her head and nibbled his way down her throat. "Taste so fucking good, Will. Like sugar cookies and strawberries."

"I thought you didn't like sweets." She ran her hand along his shoulder. The muscles rippled under her fingertips. She'd never been with someone so big. So built. Feeling him over his clothes wasn't enough. She wanted to see him, too.

He pulled back and cupped her cheek. "I like your sweetness."

She melted, any hesitation she had gone. It had been five long years without feeling a connection to a man only sex could give. Years where she'd never lost herself in someone else's touch. Even if nothing more came of this relationship, she wanted to at least remember that she'd given herself this moment.

She climbed off him and offered him her hand. She tugged him to standing and led him to her room, putting her finger over her lips as they crept past Tilda's. She locked her bedroom door then leaned against it, watching Travis.

He watched her back.

The two of them stood, a couple of feet separating them, just drinking each other in. She was the first to move. She reached for the bottom hem of his shirt and tugged it up.

Travis raised his arms to help, pulling it off over the last couple inches that she couldn't reach.

Her jaw dropped. She swallowed. She'd known he was ripped; she could tell that even through his clothes. But knowing and seeing what lay beneath were two very different things. "Wow," she breathed.

He balled up his shirt and tossed it aside. "Like what you see?"

Dumbly, she nodded. Travis's torso was a work of art. Strong pecs with just the right amount of hair, six-pack abs, and that alluring vee that dipped beneath the waist of his trousers.

Insecurities she didn't know she had flared to life. This man's body was a lethal weapon, in more ways than one. The last time she'd been to a gym was in college.

He bent and quickly shucked his socks. His boots he'd taken off when he'd entered her apartment. Willow caught a glimpse of his back, muscles she didn't even know existed flexing, before he straightened.

"Your turn." He reached for the zipper on the back of her dress. The rasp of it being lowered sent a shiver down her spine. The dress slipped off her shoulders, and she grabbed for it, holding it to her chest.

Travis stilled. "Did you change your mind?"

"No." She scraped her teeth over her bottom lip. "It's just...you're just..." She waved one hand up and down his body. "You must be used to beautiful women with hard bodies and five-percent body fat. I'm afraid you'll be disappointed."

He took off the clip that held her hair back and combed her curls out around her shoulders. "*You* are beautiful. The most beautiful woman I've ever see." He cradled the back of her neck, gently massaging. "I've had enough hard in my life, Willow. I want to lose myself in someone soft. I promise you I won't be disappointed."

His fingers, his words, the look in his eyes. It was all enough to make her relax her arms. Her dress pooled at her ankles.

Travis's eyes went half-mast. He traced the strap of her lilac satin bra down to her breast then glided his finger over the cup. He circled her nipple, never touching it, until it hardened into an aching point. "I'm the opposite of disappointed. You're a fucking pin-up fantasy."

She arched into his touch. Her matching bra and panties set did have a 1940s vibe, the high-waisted panties retro and flattering. She stopped caring what she looked like. She wanted to see more of the man in front of her. She undid the button on his pants. Wanting to protect the bulge that pressed against his zipper, she put her left hand down the inside of his pants as she lowered the zipper with her right.

His cock twitched against the back of her hand, as eager to be seen as she was to see it. She pushed his boxers down his hips with his pants until the monster he carried between his legs popped free.

"Wow," she whispered again. She cradled his cock between her hands, exploring every inch.

A muscle flicked in his jaw, but Travis let her play. She traced the veins running its length, cradled his sac, rubbed her palm over the precum leaking from his crown.

Travis's chest heaved. His hands fisted. Willow fondled him until he broke.

"That's it." He grabbed her wrists and yanked her to his body. He lowered his head until they were nose to nose. "My turn."

He spun, bringing them down on her bed. Her double mattress was too short for him, so he angled their bodies before covering her with his. Pressing her breasts together, he licked between her cleavage, growling deep in his throat. He reached behind her and popped the clasp on her bra before dragging it off.

"Jesus, Mary, and Joseph." His words were almost a prayer. "Your tits are amazing."

She smothered a snort. Men and boobs. Still, if her chest gave Travis even half as much pleasure as his body gave her, then she was happy to be well-endowed.

He sucked and nibbled on the underside of her breasts, and her amusement was drowned in waves of heat. He licked around her nipple before sucking the tip into his hot, wet mouth.

"Oh God." She pressed up, trying to get him to touch as much of her flesh as possible. Her core grasped at nothing. Sweat beaded at her temple.

He lavished equal attention on her other breast, suckling and nipping until her thighs rubbed against each other, instinctively trying to create their own friction. It was almost a relief when he moved down her body and his mouth was replaced by cool air on her aching peaks.

The relief didn't last long. He licked his way down her abdomen, scored her hips with his teeth. When he pulled her panties down, he took his pants off, too. He placed his palms on her inner thighs and pressed them apart.

His eyes flared. "Such a pretty pussy." He butterflied his fingertip down her slit. "Are you as sweet here as everywhere else?"

His face disappeared between her legs. She held her breath, the anticipation making her tense. She felt his breath on her curls. The stubble of his jaw against the tender skin of her thigh. Then finally, finally, the velvety bliss of his tongue.

He licked her from core to clit.

She just about came off the bed. Travis clamped his arm around her waist, pinning her down as he continued his assault. He plunged his tongue inside her channel as his nose rubbed against her clit.

"Oh God oh God oh God." She tugged his hair. Nothing had ever felt so good in her whole life, and she needed it to stop. "Travis." She yanked at his head again. "Up."

"What's wrong?" He bit her hip.

"Absolutely nothing except my eight-year-old daughter doesn't need her mommy screaming to wake her up." She gripped his shoulders and pulled him higher. "I can't take that right now."

He settled over her, his elbows on either side of her head. "That's cute." He crushed his mouth to hers, the kiss rough, demanding.

She blinked up at him when he pulled back, her mind going in and out of focus. "What's cute?"

One corner of his lips curled up. "That you think you won't scream with my dick inside you. Now, are we protected or do I need to suit up?"

She drew her eyebrows together. "Suit up? Oh." She slid her hands down his abdomen and gripped his shaft. "I had the birth control shot."

"That's good. And I'm clean. I get checked all the time in the military." He rolled his hips into her grip. "I want to take you bare, nothing in between us. Can I?"

Yes, she wanted that, too. She nodded and brought her knees up to his hips, opening herself.

Travis notched himself at her entrance. He made shallow, lazy thrusts, his fat head lighting up all the nerve endings at her opening but going no farther.

"Travis," she admonished. She tried to lift her hips, bring him deeper inside, but didn't have the angle to control the movements.

"Hmm?" He licked around the shell of her ear then sucked on her lobe.

Her body flushed with heat. His teasing felt so damn good while leaving her empty at the same time. "Fuck me." She wanted it to sound like a demand but it came out more a plea. Her shoulders drew toward her spine. Her legs trembled. Good God, she might actually be able to come if he kept this up long enough. But she didn't want it this way. She wanted all of him, inside her, filling her as she clutched around his girth.

"I thought you wanted something pleasant. Easy." He scraped his jaw along hers. "No screaming, remember."

She dug her nails into his ass. There was a time and place for his playfulness. This wasn't it. "I swear to all that is holy, if you don't fuck me good and hard I will make you regret it in ways you can't even imagine."

He grinned. "Did you just use your mom voice on me?"

Willow narrowed her eyes. It wasn't her mom voice. It was her getting shit done voice. And it had better work on him.

"Don't worry." He kissed the corner of her mouth before covering her lips with his palm. "I think it's sexy. Now just remember, you asked for this."

She reached up to remove his hand just as he drove deep. His palm muffled her scream, and instead of taking it off her mouth, she clutched it closer.

Sweet Jesus, she'd never felt anything like Travis. He slammed into her again, stretching her walls and stealing her breath. He rested his weight on his elbows then placed his other hand over her throat, squeezing lightly as he set up a pounding rhythm.

Willow let her eyes flutter closed. The pleasure of his thrusts ended in a sharp pinch when he bottomed out. The nip of pain melded into ecstasy as his cock dragged out of her channel, only to repeat the process over and over with each stroke.

His hands on her mouth and throat were warm and firm. She'd have thought she'd hate it if a man held her this way. It made her feel vulnerable. Stripped of control.

Instead, she kind of loved it. She didn't have to worry about controlling herself, her noises. Travis would make sure Tilda remained blissfully unaware of what her mother was getting up to across the hall. He took that burden from her. Willow was free to just enjoy the moment.

She hooked her ankles behind his back. The next time he pulled out, she clenched the muscles of her channel.

Travis cursed. He snapped his hips forward. "Open your eyes," he demanded. "I want to see the look in them when you come apart."

His gaze was filled with lust. Determination. She gripped his biceps and held on for the ride. Each slide of his cock drove her higher. Every piston of his hips coiled her muscles tighter and tighter.

But it was the look in his eyes that finally broke her. Adoration shone from their depths. He looked at her as if she was his greatest treasure.

She screamed as she shattered. Waves of rapture gathered at her core and exploded outward. Her spine curled. Her toes tingled. Travis kept rocking into her, extending her pleasure until finally, he erupted too.

He buried his face in her shoulder and bit down to muffle his own cries. Pulse after pulse of wet heat filled her sex. Her body milked him, sucking at him gently until her spasms slowed, then stopped.

She went limp. Travis covered her like a huge weighted blanket, and she couldn't remember ever feeling so content. She ran her hands along his spine, through his hair, just enjoying having a man in her arms. This man.

She'd thought she didn't have time for him in her life. She'd been an idiot. For a man like Travis, she'd make the time.

Her eyelids went heavy. She'd have to ask Travis to leave. Even though her bed would feel empty now without him, she couldn't have him here when Tilda woke.

Travis shifted. He kissed her throat where his hand had been.

In a minute. She'd ask him to leave in a minute. She yawned and snuggled closer. Right now she'd just enjoy feeling in every stretched and deliciously sore muscle just exactly how wrong she'd been.

Chapter Twelve

TRAVIS RECHECKED HIS MK 17, made sure the clip was fully loaded with a bullet in the chamber. He ran his fingers over his tactical vest, ensuring his blades were all in their proper places. Damn, he'd missed this.

His headset crackled a moment before Ryan's voice came over the line. "Skee looks nervous after his extended vacation." Ryan leaned forward from his seat on the Super Stallion. The sound of the chopper's blades was muted from their ear protection to a low throb, letting his voice ring loud and clear. Unfortunately. "It's like he's been revirginized. Don't worry. We'll go easy on you."

"Fuck off," Travis said. There was no heat to his words. He was in too good a mood to let Ryan get to him. He was back on active, taking part in his first training exercise since the injury. Things were going great with Willow. He'd spent the night twice more at her place, making sure to sneak out at oh four thirty so Tilda wouldn't catch him there. Dragging himself away from Willow's soft, curvy body wasn't fun, but he understood her need to keep Tilda unaware of what was happening in her mother's bedroom.

He sighed. Willow needed a bigger home. Someplace where the master bedroom wasn't right next to the kid's. Some place with a yard for Tilda to play in. A nice kitchen for Willow to play in. And sound proof walls so Travis could play when he got Willow alone.

"Look at that goofy smile." Tony shook his head. "He's not nervous. He's lovesick. He's been playing house too long and doesn't know what to do now that he has to go back to work."

Travis shifted in his seat. That one hit a little close to home. He was thrilled to be back working, but he had to admit he didn't like not being able to see Willow whenever the urge struck. What if Calhoun made another move against her business and Travis wasn't nearby to intervene? How the fuck did Jake and Chris manage this feeling when they went off on missions, never knowing how long they'd be separated from their women?

"How *is* it going with Willow?" Chris asked. "We didn't scare her off at the barbecue, did we? 'Cause I know Sam would like to see her again."

"No, she and Tilda had a great time." Even though Willow had been the only woman wearing a dress and heels to a backyard barbecue, she'd still fit right in. Laughing with the women, teasing the men. And Tilda hadn't lacked for entertainment. His friends had all seemed to enjoy playing with the little girl, finding bugs to make her squeal, twirling her around the yard so she flew 'like Supergirl.' In general making fools of themselves.

As if reading his mind, Ryan's voice crackled through the headset again. "The kid is cute," he said. "But aren't you worried about messing around with a single mom? Willow would probably love to snag a new daddy for Tilda."

Travis checked his watch. They were still eight minutes out from their arrival site. He could ignore Ryan for eight minutes.

What he couldn't ignore were the tiny swirls of nausea that coiled through his stomach. Because he *was* worried about being with a single mom, just not for the reason Ryan thought. None of his friends had kids yet, so he didn't know how much help they would be.

He decided to try anyway. "I hope Willow wants me to be Tilda's father. She's it for me. I knew it the moment I saw her, and the feeling has only grown as I spend time with her."

"Then what's the problem?" Jake would be the one to see he was concerned.

Travis fingered the grip on his tactical knife. "I have nieces and nephews. I like kids. But I don't know how to be a father. What if I'm crap at it?"

"Treat it like a mission." Tony shrugged. "Observe. Orient. Decide. Act. Don't fail," he added.

The OODA Loop. It was how Travis had been trained. Learn the situation, decide on the best approach, and implement the plan. He didn't know how well Willow would react if he treated her daughter like a mission, however.

Jake gripped the top of his vest. "If you care, you won't be crap at it."

Ryan groaned. "Jesus, Mary, and Joseph. We're men on a training mission, not teenage girls braiding hair and gossiping about the cute boy in class. We're each holding deadly weapons and are about to go shoot some shit up. Can we act like it, please?"

Everyone ignored him. Jake readjusted a strap on his tactical vest. "I might be able to tell you more about parenthood in a couple months."

That shut even Ryan up. The chopper went silent except for the soft *whomp whomp* of the blades.

"You knock Caroline up?" Ryan finally asked.

"Not yet." Jake scanned the terrain out the window before turning back to them. "But now that we've set a date for the wedding, I'm trying to put a baby in her." His eyes glowed with contentment. "The wedding is the first weekend in November, by the way. You all better be there."

Shit. A wedding. A baby. Their Element Leader's life had changed dramatically in a few short months. Travis had to respect the man. Jake had found the woman for him and wasted no time in locking her down. If only Travis could be so lucky.

He wondered what Willow's pregnancy with Tilda had been like. Had she been sick a lot? Had her husband rubbed her tired feet? Held her hand through the labor? Travis wanted to see her round with his child. Wanted to discover everything he'd missed with Tilda.

And he needed to keep these thoughts to himself for a while longer. He could only imagine that Willow would panic if she knew all the plans he had for them. Although taking it to the next level felt natural for him, it was too soon for Willow. He had to play this right. He couldn't lose her.

"A dad," he said to Jake, shaking his head. "I think our missions would be easier."

"Probably." Jake shrugged. "But when you find the right woman, the path forward becomes clear."

Travis bit the inside of his cheek. His path was clear. To him. He just needed to convince Willow. Getting her to accept that he was the man for her was one thing. It was a huge leap of faith for a single mom to let a man into her daughter's life, however. He'd make a good start. Willow had let him past so many of her walls, but he had a feeling he needed to step it up.

The helicopter hovered over a patch of forest where the trees had thinned. "It's go time," Jake said. He opened the door, and wind whipped into the space. He attached two fifty-foot cables to the hooks in the floor of the chopper and kicked the ends out the door.

"Ready to rappel?" he asked.

"Oorah." Ryan was the first to attach his carabiner to the cable. "See you on the ground," he said, then stepped out of the helicopter.

Travis checked his gear one last time. His mind focused on the training op ahead. Observe. Orient. Decide. Act. When he and his squad used those tactics, they succeeded.

He attached his carabiner, gripped the cable, and waited for a nod from Jake. He jumped into space. His heart kicked up a notch as he made his controlled descent to the ground.

There was no reason he couldn't succeed with Willow. All he had to do was use his training.

Chapter Thirteen

THE BILL WOULDN'T PUT her in the red for this month, but it would be close. Willow stared at her accounting program, then the bill with the hefty penalty from the IRS, then back at her computer. She sat at the small desk wedged into the shop's kitchen and wondered where she had gone wrong. With the payroll tax return. With her business.

With her life.

She sighed heavily. If the federal payroll tax return was wrong, dollars to donuts the state return was wrong, as well. There was nothing for it. She'd have to file an amended return. Another task to add to her ever increasing to-do list.

Something nudged the toe of her pump. She looked down to see a marble careening lazily away from her foot.

She rubbed her forehead. "Please don't play with marbles in the shop," she told Tilda for the thousandth time. "That's an accident waiting to happen." She couldn't have Mandi breaking her ankle. Aside from the fact she'd hate to see her hurt, her worker's comp insurance would go through the roof.

Tilda scooted along the floor and grabbed for the marble. "When can we go to the library? You said I could borrow a movie."

"Maybe in a little while." Willow forced a smile for her daughter.

Tilda bounced her marble on the wood floor. "Jenny taught me a new game at recess today. Wanna play? I can teach it to you."

Her temple began to throb. "I'm sorry, baby, but I'm busy right now. Maybe later."

"You're always busy." Tilda threw her marble at the wall. It ricocheted off the panel and rolled under the refrigerator.

"That wasn't too smart." Willow tried to keep her voice even. "Now you're down a marble." There was no way she was muscling her fridge out to retrieve the damn thing. Maybe next deep clean.

"Like I care." Her daughter scowled.

"Hey." Willow turned her chair to face her daughter as her phone buzzed. She snapped it up, grateful for the reprieve. She couldn't let Tilda get away with the attitude, but she also couldn't blame her daughter for being mad at her. There had been so many broken promises on Willow's end. Days at the park that had never happened. Board game nights that had turned into Tilda watching TV alone.

She was screwing up as a parent. She knew it. She also knew Tilda had to eat and get new clothes each year. But little girls didn't understand the compromises their moms had to make.

The text was from Travis. *Been thinking about you. How's your day going?*

God, she was tempted to unload on him. Tell him just how crappy the day was treating her, get some sympathy. But that would only take up more time, time that she didn't have. She put her phone down on the desk. When she was with Travis, everything was amazing. He made her remember who she was before bills and greedy developers and parent teacher conferences got in the way. She liked who she was with Travis. And she really liked him.

She nibbled on her lower lip and looked at the phone. No. She turned back to the computer. No time for texting.

"We have to be at your school in three hours." She rolled her head around on her neck. "Maybe we can stop at the library beforehand." Tonight was the school's open house. Tilda's teacher had made a point of asking Willow to come by and speak to her.

"Maybe, maybe, maybe," Tilda muttered. "That means no."

Willow's shoulders drew back. She barely managed to keep from snapping at Tilda. She was the adult. She needed to keep her cool.

Especially when Tilda was right. Maybe usually did mean no when Willow said it. Something pinched behind her breastbone, and she rubbed at it.

Mandi stepped through the kitchen door. "The front is empty right now." She fidgeted with the end of her ponytail. "I was hoping I could talk with you?"

"Sure." Willow leaned closer to her computer screen. What was that number doing there? "What's up?"

"Uh, I know the timing of this isn't great, but I'm moving."

Willow blinked, then slowly turned to look at her employee.

"In a month," Mandi said. When Willow still didn't say anything, she added, "So, I can't work for you anymore after that."

Willow just stared at her, numbness sweeping through her limbs.

"Where are you going?" Tilda asked, breaking the silence.

"Durham." Mandi shifted. "My boyfriend got accepted to a graduate program at Duke. He asked me to go with him."

It was a big step in Mandi's relationship. Willow knew this, but still she wanted to protest. Stomp her feet and tell the girl no. Basically, she wanted to have a Tilda-sized tirade about how unfair life was being.

Instead, she stood and strode to Mandi. "Congratulations." She gave her a hug. The girl's shoulders sagged. "You must be so excited."

"Yeah." Mandi gave her a squeeze then stepped back, a relieved smile on her face. "I thought you'd be mad at me."

"I'm disappointed to be losing my favorite employee—"

"Your only employee," Mandi pointed out.

As if Willow needed the reminder. And now she'd have to hire two new people. Train two new people. Her cheeks ached with the strain of keeping her lips curved up. "But I'm happy for you. We'll have to have a farewell party for you before you go."

"Sounds good."

Willow's phone rattled on top of the desk. She turned back for it. Another text from Travis. *How about dinner tonight? I can bring something over for the three of us.*

She dropped her head, closing her eyes. A part of her really wanted to see him.

The other part, the one that kept her schedules and to-do lists, saw him as someone else who needed her time and energy.

After the school's open house, Willow needed to get some work done. With Travis over at her place so often, she'd fallen even further behind.

The backs of her eyes burned. Exhaustion swept over her. She wanted nothing more than to crawl into bed and pull the covers over her head.

She'd just started typing, telling him maybe another time, when an explosion sounded in the front, followed by a shower of broken glass.

All three of them jumped, then looked at the kitchen door, wide-eyed.

Willow crept to the door, pushed it open a crack, and peered out. A cool breeze wafted over her face, and her eyes zeroed in on the source of the draft. She pushed the door wider and gaped at the damage.

"What...?" Mandi peered over her shoulder. "Holy cow. The entire window is gone."

Along with the tower of jams displayed in front of it. "Stay behind the counter," she told Mandi and Tilda as she shuffled forward. Shards of broken glass littered the floor of the shop. Jam dripped onto the wooden planks from the jars that had broken on the ground. And leaning on the leg of one of the tables, a fat red brick lay.

Willow crunched over glass to get to it. She picked it up. BITCH was written in big, straight letters in black ink on the side of it.

Her hand shook. Carefully, she placed the brick back where she'd found it and straightened. She smoothed her hands down the front of her dress. "Mandi, will you take Tilda upstairs? Stay with her until I get this cleaned up?" Her voice was dull. Toneless.

Something in it must have made Mandi keep any of her usual snarky commentary to herself. "Of course." She took Tilda's hand and the two of them skirted around the mess and to the front door. "Let me know if you need any help."

Willow nodded. Her stomach felt like it was filled with lead. She pressed her hand to her abdomen. She had to call her insurance. Call the police. Call a glazier. Close the store. Clean the mess up.

She called the police first. After she reported it, she decided to gather the supplies she'd need for clean-up so she could start right after they took pictures and left. She shambled down the hall to her supply closet. The window repair man probably wouldn't be able to come out on such short notice. She'd need to board it up. Where would she find window-sized boards? How would they fit in her little car?

She pulled the closet door open and blinked at the dark interior. She couldn't see anything. She squeezed her forehead between her thumb and forefinger. Oh, yeah. The light. She turned it on and looked for the broom.

After she found it, she held tight to the handle. She didn't want to go back out front. Didn't want to see yet another mess she had to deal with. She rested her forehead on the shelf in front of her.

And then she cried.

Chapter Fourteen

THE POLICE CRUISER PARKED in front of *It's Your Jam* made Travis's pulse rocket. He hurried to the door and burst inside.

Willow stood with a broom in her hand and a pile of glass at her feet. A uniformed officer was next to her, a small notepad and pen in his hand. They both looked up at his entrance.

Willow's eyes lit up before her forehead creased. "What are you doing here?"

Travis eyed the space where the window used to be, the broken jam jars, and the brick nestled inside a plastic evidence bag that lay on a display table. The word BITCH was clearly legible on the red stone. The back of his neck went hot. "You didn't text or call me back. I was worried." He circled the mess and wrapped Willow in his arms, squeezing her to his body.

Her muscles tensed before relaxing against him. "Thanks," she whispered. "I was going to call you back, but then this happened and I had to call the police, my insurance, someone to replace the window..."

Her voice warbled, and Travis's rage shot to new heights. Willow was a strong woman, but she sounded like she might be reaching her breaking point. Obviously, his message to Calhoun hadn't been strong enough. He couldn't wait to remedy that.

Rubbing her back, he turned to the cop. "Do we know who did this? Did you see who threw the brick?" he asked Willow.

She shook her head. "I told him about Beau Calhoun, but I don't know if he did this. It...it doesn't feel like his style."

The officer flipped his notebook shut and slid it in his breast pocket. "Mr. Calhoun is friends with the mayor and very active in our local economy. I'll have a talk with him, but without evidence there isn't much that can be done." There wasn't much the police would do, was the implication.

Travis pressed his lips together but nodded. The officer was just being realistic, and a brick through a window wasn't the crime of the century.

"I'll include this street on our local patrols," the cop said to Willow. He picked up the brick. "If we're able to pull any prints off of this, I'll have you come down to the station to have yours taken for elimination."

"Thank you." She pulled from Travis's arms and escorted the officer out of the shop. She leaned back against the door.

"Are you okay?" Two pedestrians paused at the empty window, peering inside curiously. Travis glared at them until they moved along.

"I'm fine." Willow's wobbly smile showed her words were a lie. She shoved off the door and went behind the counter for a garbage can. She brought it to the pile of debris. "I'm sorry I can't do dinner tonight. There's so much I need to do, and getting this window replaced is just the tip of the iceberg. Of course, the glazier can't come out until tomorrow so I need to run to the hardware store for some wood to board it up. I need to—"

Travis took the broom and dustpan from her clenched hands. He set them aside and took her in his arms again.

She felt so good pressed against him. Her soft curves were the perfect balance to his hardness. He hated the small tremors that went through her body, but he was glad he was here to hold her through them. "It's going to be all right," he murmured into her hair. "You'll get through this. Whatever I can do to help, I will."

She sighed. "I don't even know if this is all worth it anymore. I thought having my own shop was the answer to everything. I wouldn't have a boss to answer to and I could see Tilda whenever I wanted." She wrapped her arms around his waist. "It hasn't worked out like I expected."

"You're going through some rough waters right now, but there are clear skies up ahead. I promise."

She huffed out a soft laugh. "An ocean metaphor? Maybe you should have been a SEAL."

He gave her butt a soft swat. "Don't even joke about that. A Frogman could only dream of being a Raider."

"A little competition between the branches, huh?' She smiled up at him, and this time the smile was genuine.

Because her lips were right there, he lowered his head and pressed a quick kiss to them. "Sweetness, the SEALs are no competition to us," he quipped. He breathed her in. She smelled like oranges today, and he guessed she'd been making marmalade. "Why don't you think Calhoun did this?" he asked quietly.

She shrugged. "He's been a pain in the butt, but he's never been...malicious. That brick, it felt like whoever threw that really hated me. But I guess that's silly. Who else would do something like this?"

"Don't discount your instincts." Too many people did that. Though Travis hoped this time her instincts were wrong. Calhoun he could deal with. Travis didn't like the idea of someone unknown lurking about who had a grudge against Willow.

She stepped back and examined her shop. "Time to get back to work." Her gaze locked on the clock on the wall above the kitchen door. Her shoulders slumped. "I should be going to the open house at Tilda's school right about now. I guess it will have to wait until another day for her teacher to tell me all the ways Tilda isn't paying attention in class."

"Go." Travis started scooping the broken jars into the dustpan and dumping them in the garbage. "I'll take care of cleaning up and getting the window boarded. In fact, why don't you leave Tilda here with me. She can help me and you can have one-on-one time with her teacher."

Willow dug her teeth into her bottom lip. "You don't have to do that."

He knotted the plastic bag lining the garbage can and stood. He did have to do this. That was something Willow would have to learn about him. For now, he simply said, "I want to do this. Don't worry. Do what you need to do. I've got everything here."

She fiddled with the button of her navy dress. Her doubt was a physical thing, and Travis couldn't deny that it stung. He'd hoped she'd known she could count on him by now, but perhaps he was expecting too much. Tonight would be a good opportunity to show her.

"I understand if you want to take Tilda with you," he said, "but trust me with your shop. I'll get it sorted."

"It would be nice to speak with Tilda's teacher alone." She shifted on her heels. "All right. I'll go get Tilda and bring her down here. We were supposed to go to the library to borrow a movie...."

"If me and the guys get the window boarded up early, I'll take her."

Willow blinked in surprise. "You don't have—"

"—to do that. I know." Travis went to her and ran his hand up and down her arm. "Trust me, I'm not doing anything I don't want to. Now go. I've got this."

"Okay." She pulled open the door. Hesitated. "Well, thank you. I'll, uh, go bring Tilda down then head out. Call me if anything—"

"We'll be fine." He patted her bottom. And because it felt so nice, he patted it again. "Go."

He pulled out his phone when she'd left and texted Chris what he needed. He knew his friends would be over as soon as they could and the window would be boarded in no time. Travis hadn't realized how reassuring it was to have people you could call on, day or night, and know they'd be there until he'd seen Willow's uncertainty. She didn't have that in her life, not until now.

He was going to be that person for Willow. The one she could depend on, no matter what.

He only had to convince her of it.

Chapter Fifteen

"THE VIDEO IS SAVED for two weeks," Travis told her as they walked through her shop. It was after closing the next day. Willow still didn't have a window, the glazier having pushed the job off until tomorrow, but she did have cameras. Cameras that seemed to record every inch of her shop except the inside of the bathroom.

She didn't quite know how she felt about it.

"After two weeks, it's automatically wiped unless you put in a request to save it." Travis reached up to adjust the angle on one of the cameras, his T-shirt rising with the motion and exposing his washboard abs.

Her mouth watered, but she would not be distracted. "And how much does all this cost?"

"The cameras were an upfront cost, and the company charges one-fifty a year for its service." He rested his palms on her shoulders. "But don't worry. I'm paying for it."

"One-hundred fifty plus the cameras." Willow blew out a breath. That was actually fairly reasonable. She only wished Travis had consulted her about it. She'd been busy helping a client when he'd arrived this afternoon. After a quick kiss, he'd set about installing them. There were five cameras in all. One was in the front of the shop, one in the kitchen, and one in the hallway that led to the bathroom and rear exit. Two were outside, front and back. If anyone tried to break another window or clog another toilet, he would be seen.

"Okay, but I'm paying," she said. "Give me the bill and I'll reimburse you."

"Willow—"

She held up her hand. "You're not going to be paying for my business."

"I'm paying for your safety." Travis crossed his arms over his chest. "Besides, this is more for me than it is for you. It will keep me from worrying about you constantly."

"It's a tax deduction for me." She headed for the kitchen, clearing an abandoned plate from one of the tables on the way. She was going to pay for this, even if she had to sneak the money into his wallet. This was her business, her responsibility.

His footsteps followed her to the sink. "I know you wouldn't have got cameras on your own. You're not responsible—"

She spun. "I am responsible for everything that happens in my shop." In her life. "Look, it was sweet what you did. And I'm grateful. I'm also not a pauper. I know I bitch and moan about *It's Your Jam*, but it's doing okay. I can pay my own bills, money isn't the problem." Money was tight and always on the verge of being a problem, but she was afloat. She rinsed the plate and stuck it in the dishwasher. "It's everything else about running the business I hate," she muttered.

He laid his hand on her hip. The heat from his body warmed her back. She stilled. It would feel so good to lean back against him. Maybe ask if he could massage away some of her tension. Maybe give him a little bit of her problems to share.

But she had so many balls up in the air, she was sure to drop them all if she tried to give away one or two.

"You're going to let me help you, Will." He rested his chin on top of her head, his palm sliding around to her belly. "I would have no idea how to help you make jam, or bake, or do the accounting, but I know security. And I know how to protect what's mine."

His. The very idea made her stomach flutter and twist and in general behave like a baby bunny. It wasn't an altogether comfortable feeling. She wasn't eager to make it stop, though, either.

"After my latest talk with Calhoun, I don't think you'll have more problems with him. The cameras are just a precaution."

She turned and leaned back against the sink to look in his eyes. "What?"

"I think you might be right that he didn't throw the brick." Travis scrubbed a hand over his face. "He was genuinely surprised."

"No, I meant what were you doing talking to Calhoun? Again? Travis, this is my business, my—"

He pressed a finger to her lips. "We're going to have to reach a compromise here. If someone is hassling you, I'm going to have a talk with them. That's not changing. Maybe you could let me be the muscle of the relationship and you can be the brains."

Her lips twitched against his finger. He shouldn't want her to be the brains of the relationship. That organ told her to stay mad, that he had overreached.

But she was tired of being angry. Tired of being stressed. And a damn fine bit of muscle was standing before her.

She kissed his skin, let her tongue come out and play. "I can make that compromise." She sucked gently at the tip of his finger.

His eyes flared with hunger. He pushed his finger into her mouth, slowly retreated, before doing it all again. "You are the sexiest woman I know, Willow Janna."

She didn't think she'd ever been someone's sexiest woman. Her husband's sexiest had been a movie star, and that was okay because the woman was smoking hot.

Travis pulled his finger free and put his hands to much better use. They molded over her curves, skimming up her waist to cup her breasts. "What you do to me, Willow. The filthy thoughts you give me." He brushed his thumbs over her nipples. "You can't imagine all the ways I want to use your body. I want to fuck you so hard you won't be able to stand. Your legs will be like jelly."

She dropped her head back. God, yes, she wanted that too. Under his hands, her body was already feeling like....

She blinked. Damn. "I can't right now." She put her hands on his chest, meaning to push him away but her fingers curled into his shirt instead. "I have three batches of jam to make tonight," she said regretfully. "I cancelled my canning class because of everything that's been going on, but I kept the sitter for Tilda. I should use it to work."

He dropped his forehead onto her shoulder and groaned. "Always so responsible." But the smile he gave her said he didn't mind. "Can I help?"

She circled around him and started gathering ingredients. "Didn't you say you couldn't help me make jam?" she teased. "That you were only good for your muscle?"

"You know damn well that's not the only thing I'm good for." He rubbed her butt before giving it a little tap.

Her nipples pebbled. Travis seemed to have a fondness for giving her ass love pats, and she couldn't say she didn't like it, too. Before her mind went somewhere that would distract her completely, she asked, "So how's your work going? What's it like being back?"

She hated the scar on his thigh. Hated that at any moment in his job he could get hurt. Or worse. But the way his eyes lit up when he talked about what he did made her heart warm. Travis did what he loved. There wasn't one part of his career he didn't seem to like. She was a bit jealous.

"It's great. I got to repel from a helicopter this week and next week we're doing joint training with the Navy working on marine maneuvers." He pushed the jar of sugar over to her when she pointed. "I'm just glad I'm back for the guys. Being down a man on the squad isn't easy."

She tossed the cut pineapple and coconut into her jam pot and stirred. "When do you think you'll leave on a...?"

"Mission?"

She nodded, the back of her throat thick. The thought of him flying off into unknown danger while she waited at home, having no idea where he was going or what he was doing, made her queasy. She'd been spoiled having so much time with him when he was on medical leave. And she'd spent half that time pushing him away.

Maybe she should have done a better job of pushing. Then she wouldn't have to worry when he did leave.

"I don't know." He watched her add rum to the mix, his eyebrow raising. "I never know. But when I do leave, the men from the other squads will be around to watch over you. I'll leave you with their phone numbers. You can call them for anything."

She dropped the spoon. "It's not me I'm worried about."

"I know." The corners of his eyes crinkled. "I'll be worrying about you and you'll be worrying about me. And none of it does anyone any good."

And yet they'd still worry. She carried the pot to the stove and turned the heat to medium-high.

Travis was right behind her. "You done?"

"Done combining it, yes." She slid a baking sheet laden with empty glass jars into the oven. "But I have to— eep!"

Travis wrapped his arms around her waist, pulling her back to his chest, and spun them around. He marched them to the clean end of her worktable and bent her over the flat surface. "While that heats up, how about we cook up a little something right here?" His lips curved against the back of her neck.

Willow rolled her eyes at his cheesy line, but she couldn't help her grin. It had been so long since she'd just had fun, and Travis brought that in spades. "We have ten minutes until that jam starts to burn. Hardly enough time for the main event, plus a warm-up and cool down." She wiggled her butt against the front of his jeans. The hard bulge behind the denim ground against her core, and she rocked onto her toes to increase the friction.

Really, her warm-up was already done. It didn't take long for her body to get ready when Travis was around. Sweet, yet commanding, he was the perfect combination to rev her engines. But still she continued to tease him. "You do know how I like to stretch before and after a workout."

He slid his palms up the back of her legs, a cool draft following as he lifted her skirt. "Don't worry. What I'm about to do will stretch you out real good."

Willow stopped smiling when his hand met the apex of her thighs. She closed her eyes on a soft moan. Any thoughts of the cooking, the cleaning up she needed to do, evaporated like mist in the desert.

He cupped her possessively as he licked around the rim of her ear. "You have no fucking clue what you do to me, do you?"

She pressed her hips back, and his hard bulge nestled between her cheeks. She bit her lip. "I have some idea."

The belt of her apron pulled tight as Travis tucked her skirt under its bow. "Any two people can have sex. This is more than that." He rocked his hand up and his fingertip skated over her clit.

She rolled onto her toes, the feeling almost too good. The gusset of her panties clung wetly to her lower lips. This did feel like more somehow, but it also wasn't making love, not with her bent over her worktable.

It felt like a claiming.

He slid her panties down her legs, lifting her ankles to help her step out of them. He gripped the cheeks of her ass a moment before his tongue eased between her folds.

Willow gripped the opposite edge of the table. "Oh God, yes." Her mind scattered. She couldn't feel any part of her body except where his mouth touched. It was like all her nerve endings knew where the good stuff was happening and fled to take up residence in her pussy.

He nibbled on her outer lips as he traced a figure eight with his finger, around her clit, to her opening, and back again. "I picked the right time to install the cameras. This will be so hot to watch on replay."

The cameras. Shit. The part of her brain that was still thinking told her to stand up and fix her skirt. She didn't need her butt featured in film. The other part of her brain, the side that reacted on instinct, rocked her hips back into his face. This felt too damn good to stop. "No one can see this."

The pads of his fingers dug into her flesh, massaging her backside even as his wicked tongue made everything inside her go tight. He nipped at the fleshy part of her ass, where her cheek met her thigh. "Only you can request the video feed. No one will see it if you don't want." He stood. His zipper sounded then the head of his cock trailed up and down her crease. "I think you should watch it, though. I have an amazing view right now."

He pushed in an inch, pulled out.

Her knuckles ached with how hard she clasped the table's edge. She usually adored Travis's playfulness, but there was a time and place for everything. "Please," she whimpered.

"Does my sweetness need something? You want my dick to split you wide?" His voice was low and dirty and made her whole body flush.

"Please," she repeated. She was reduced to a one word vocabulary.

Travis gripped her hips and pushed in on one long, smooth glide. He held still inside her, his hands digging into her skin so hard she knew they'd leave bruises.

He didn't give her any space to thrust back, so she settled on wriggling her hips. "Move." Having him inside of her but keeping still was a special kind of torture.

"I can't." His voice was tight. "Watching your pussy swallow my cock almost made me blow my load. Give me a sec."

The edges of her lips curled. She liked the idea that she drove this man to the edge of control. She clutched at his length, squeezing her core muscles tight.

He let out a strangled groan. "Brat," he said before slapping her ass.

This time she clenched involuntarily, the sting of his palm spiking her need.

Finally, he began to move. Neither of them lasted long. The kitchen was filled with the sounds of skin clapping on skin, his grunts, her moans. Travis slid his hand around her hip, rubbed her clit between two fingers, and she was gone. Travis was only a moment behind.

She lay panting on the table, Travis slumped over her. Her body felt floaty and buzzed, like she'd just downed three shots of tequila. "It keeps getting better," she whispered. Even she could hear the wonder in her voice.

"And it will keep getting better. Every damn time."

She really didn't see how that was possible but decided to let him keep his illusions. She dragged in a deep breath. "That was so hot I think we started a fire." She chuckled. Then sniffed. "Shit! That's real smoke."

The fire alarm went off as Travis pulled from her body. Willow hurried to the stove, but it was too late. Her jam was a burnt mess.

Travis pulled her skirt free from the apron before grabbing her pot and quickly dumping it in the sink. He sprayed water on it. "Sorry," he yelled, wincing. "I'm responsible for that jam disaster, too. Where's a broom?" he asked over the piercing shriek of the alarm.

She pointed, and he got to work waving the smoke away from the sensor. Willow opened the back door. The burnt batch of jam was a waste of ingredients and a waste of time, two things she hated.

She leaned against the wall and looked at Travis. He'd flipped the broom around and was now jabbing at the alarm with the handle. It came off the wall, and he plucked the battery out. He smiled gleefully when the alarm cut off, like he'd just done battle and come out victorious.

Her heart fluttered. She couldn't bring herself to regret it.

Chapter Sixteen

THE MEN FROM FIRE Station 6 were good guys. Courteous, professional, and easy-going, once they realized there was no threat of a fire. Travis eyed the grizzled fire marshal taking notes in Willow's kitchen. Well, most of the firemen anyway.

Just as Travis and Willow had cleared all the smoke from the jam disaster, the engine had pulled to the front of her shop, sirens blaring. Willow's smile had dropped, and no matter how many mini-backrubs he gave her, or jokes he told to lighten the mood, it had yet to make a reappearance.

"Seriously, who calls the fire department over a household fire alarm?" Willow threw her hands up. "They go off over burnt toast. You guys must be out on a call every second of the day."

Travis squeezed her shoulder. He hated how tense she'd become. "It's okay," he murmured in her ear. "No harm, no foul."

The fire marshal swaggered over to them. "Perhaps your neighbor remembers what happened two months ago. It's no surprise she has an itchy dialing finger."

"What happened two months ago?" Travis asked. He didn't like the looks passing between Willow and Marshal Williams. These two had a history, one Willow wasn't fond of.

She huffed out a breath. "A customer smoked in the bathroom and tossed her butt into the trashcan while it was still warm. It wasn't a big deal."

"It was a fire." The marshal hooked a thumb in his wide belt and glared.

"A tiny one." Willow looked up at Travis. "Mandi called 9-1-1 before I got the extinguisher from the kitchen and put it out. The only damage was the trashcan and a little bit of the wall I had to repaint."

"And it's just that sort of lackadaisical attitude that resulted in four rounds of inspections before I would sign off on you opening your business." Williams nodded to the firemen and they started to filter out, a couple of them giving Travis and Willow sympathetic looks as they went. "You're wasting a lot of our time and resources, missy."

Willow's face went red.

Travis gently put her behind him. If she was going to blow, he wanted a barrier between her and the man who could shut down her shop. "I've been meaning to get myself one of those word-of-the-day calendars, too. I do admire a man who can use the word lackadaisical in an actual conversation." Admire, mock, it was a fine line.

Williams raked his hand through his steel-gray hair, eyes narrowing. "Miz Janna, you had a plethora of code violations that had to be cleared up before you could open."

Travis ground his jaw. Okay, now the asshole was just showing off.

"And now another accident," the fire marshal said with a sneer. "Clean up your act. I don't want to see you again." Clutching a clipboard to his wide stomach, he stomped toward the front of the shop.

Travis wrapped his arm around Willow's waist before she could follow the guy out of her kitchen. "Let him have the last word. Men like him need it to feel important."

She shrugged out of his grip. "And what about what I need."

He cocked his head. "I assume you *don't* need him ordering another round of inspections. Discretion truly is the better part of valor."

She strode to the sink and started filling it with soapy water. "You were joking with the man. That is not how I wanted to handle him."

Travis stood next to her and took the scrub brush from her hand, placing it on the counter. She was going to pull a muscle with the force she was using to scour the pot. "If I can resolve a situation with humor, I'll do everything in my power to make that happen. Because once a situation escalates to where force is necessary, it gets ugly." He held her face in his hands, needing her to understand this. "I'm very good at doing ugly, Willow. I'm trained to be brutal where needed. But there are consequences to that, and, frankly, I don't want you to see that side of me."

Her eyebrows drew together. "You seem to expect a lot from me without wanting to give all of yourself."

"Willow...."

She gripped his wrists. "No, I get it. I don't particularly want to see you killing people, either."

He ran his thumb along her cheekbone. She was so soft, yet so damned determined. He smiled. "Marshal Williams wasn't quite at the level of needing to be put down, but let me know when your next annual inspection is. If he puts the screws on you, he just might feel the full wrath of a Marine Raider."

Her lips twitched. He thought she might roll onto her toes, give him a kiss. Maybe slap his shoulder and tell him he was an idiot. But the moment passed, her amusement faded, and she pulled back.

She left her pot to soak and wiped her hands on a dishtowel. "It's getting late. I need to go up and spend time with Tilda."

"Can I join you?" He wouldn't mind seeing the little imp, either. Something about the girl's crooked, little smile had wormed its way under his skin. And he wanted every second he could get with Willow.

She shook her head. "Tilda and I need some one-on-one time."

His gut hardened. What she said was perfectly reasonable, but there was something else there. "What aren't you saying?"

"I just...I need some space." She swallowed. "You're over-whelming, Travis. I went from being too busy to date to you in my life in what feels like moments."

He leaned back against the counter and crossed his arms. "And is having me in your life a bad thing?"

"No." She rubbed the nape of her neck. "You know I like you, but maybe there are some parts of my life you don't belong in."

He kept his breathing even. That was bullshit. He wanted in everywhere. They fit. He knew it, and he suspected she did, too. This was fear talking. "Care to elaborate?"

She spread her hands out wide. "This is my business. Mine. When I have problems, they're mine to solve. And when there's a blustering fire inspector giving me grief in my shop, I'll deal with him as I see fit."

"You can't expect me to sit back if I see a problem I can fix."

"I can and I do." She untied her apron and yanked it off. "I need to be an equal partner in a relationship. I won't let you walk all over me."

"What you mean is you need everything to be on your terms." He pushed off the counter and prowled toward her. "I care for you, Willow." He'd almost used the L-word. He'd have seen nothing but a trail of dust as she sprinted away if he had. "I just want to take care of you."

She looked at the floor. "It's late, and I still have a lot to do. I'll talk to you later, okay?"

He flexed his hand. Life used to be simple. He managed any issues that came up easily. In a straightforward manner. Something broke, he fixed it. He was feeling hunger, he fed it.

Willow was determined to make it hard. She didn't seem to like simple solutions. He was there for her now; she could come to him for anything. Was it ego, pride, or fear that kept her so independent?

He gently held her shoulders and pressed a kiss to her forehead. "I'll go. And I'll be back to see you tomorrow." She needed to know she wouldn't chase him away. "Lock up after me," he told her.

She nodded and silently followed him into the front of the shop.

Travis had come on strong. He knew this. He waited to hear the click of the lock on the shop before striding to his Jeep. He'd pursued Willow with a single-minded focus she most likely wasn't used to.

He unlocked his vehicle and slid inside. This was a period of adjustment for Willow. She would adapt. Once she accepted that she could depend on him, all her attempts to push him away would come to an end.

They had to.

Because Travis couldn't imagine moving on with his life if she wasn't in it.

Chapter Seventeen

WILLOW UNLOCKED HER CAR and slid inside. She dropped her head back on the headrest and sagged into the seat. The meeting with Principal Harker had gone better than she could have hoped. The man had agreed that boredom might be Tilda's problem in class and had set up some testing to see if she qualified for the gifted program.

Her phone beeped with an incoming message. She'd ignored it during the meeting, but pulled the phone from her purse now to check.

Travis. Four messages in an hour. She smiled at the first one. Even knowing that she'd been avoiding him for the past couple days, he'd sent her a meme to make her laugh. Her smile dropped at the last message.

Sorry, she texted back. *Busy tonight. I'll let you know when I'm available*. Her thumb hovered over the send button. A big part of her didn't want to press it. She'd wanted to give herself time to think things through, but she'd missed him these last few nights.

She sent the message. She'd fallen behind on so much work, even if she'd wanted to, she shouldn't see him tonight. Her one employee was leaving in a couple of weeks and she hadn't even started looking for a replacement.

The battery icon was near empty, and she plugged it in. Nothing. She wiggled the charger, found the right angle, and jammed the phone in the cup holder so there would be pressure between the phone and charger. She shook her head and started her car. She really needed to get a new charger. Or a new phone. The battery had a life span of a gnat. Maybe if profits were good she'd get one next month.

Her phone beeped again. She waited until a red light before checking it.

Jake, Chris, and their girls are going to dinner at that seafood restaurant in Swansboro. The one right on the beach. We're almost in town now. You and Tilda have to eat. Join us.

She loved that restaurant. And a stroll on the beach afterwards with Travis by her side sounded like something that should be on her to-do list. But she'd told him she was busy and needed space and he was being pushy. She sent him a negative response and started driving again.

She turned the radio up and tried to sing along. She should feel good. She was in control. She'd asserted herself when Travis had become too presumptuous. So why did she feel empty instead?

Her heart thumped at his next message. *On my way to your shop. We're going to talk.*

There he was being bossy again. She chewed on the inside of her cheek. That side of him annoyed her almost as much as it gave her a tiny thrill.

She was going to see Travis again. Maybe she had been a little inflexible wanting to slow down their relationship?

She turned onto her street. The owner of the rock and mineral store waved to her as he closed up.

Her wave back was distracted. She peered through the windshield. Dark gray smoke billowed up in the sky near the end of the street. Her heart stalled. She stamped on the accelerator and flew the remaining blocks, praying the smoke came from anywhere but *It's Your Jam*.

"Oh, my God." She rocketed through the last three blocks and screeched to a stop next to a crowd of people huddled in the street. Her hands fumbled on the seatbelt, wasting precious seconds.

"Mandi," she screamed when she jumped out of her car. She sprinted to her employee, narrowly avoiding another vehicle pulling up. Flames danced behind the windows of her shop. She grabbed Mandi's arm. "Where's Tilda?"

The blood drained from the girl's face. "I thought she was with you," she whispered hoarsely.

"Dear God." The owner of the neighboring soap shop hugged Mandi's shoulders.

Willow spun, aiming for the door that led up to their apartment. An arm wrapped around her waist, pulling her up short. She writhed in the grip, kicking back with her heels.

"It's me." Travis held her tighter. "You can't go in there."

"Tilda!" She didn't know if she was screaming an invocation for her daughter to appear or telling Travis why he needed to let her go. Likely a bit of both.

His body went hard behind her. "Where? Shop or apartment?"

Willow had left her daughter finishing a puzzle in their apartment, with the understanding Tilda would go down to the shop when she was done to hang out with Mandi. But Mandi would have seen her if she'd gone down. "Apartment." She yanked at his hand, trying to pull free.

"Stay here. I'll get her." Travis let her go, only to grab her up again when she launched herself toward the door. He passed her to another man. "Hold her." He ran for the apartment door, disappearing inside with one of his friends following.

Jake. Jake was with him, going into the fire.

When she twisted to try to claw the face of the man stopping her from getting to Tilda, she saw Chris was also there. Caroline and Sam stood behind them, looking at the building with horror.

"Easy." Chris took her arms and pinned them to her side. "Travis and Jake will get her."

Sirens wailed faintly in the distance, an echo to the sound her heart was making. What if Tilda wasn't in the apartment? What if she was in the shop's bathroom? Mandi wouldn't have seen her there.

She threw her head back, striking a hard surface.

Chris swore and adjusted his hold.

She aimed her heel at his foot.

He yelped and lifted her off the ground so she had no leverage. "It will be okay," Chris said, making a promise he couldn't know would come true. "Let them work. Travis and Jake know what they're doing."

They might make a living rescuing people, but this was her daughter. Her heart. And these men were keeping them apart.

All the time she'd spent worrying. About her business. About her and Travis. Tilda's school. It all seemed so stupid now.

A loud crack sounded, part of the roof falling in.

Pain arced through Willow's chest. Her breath grew short, choppy. She kicked, she twisted, she screamed, but Chris didn't let her go.

The building burned.

And Willow couldn't get to her daughter.

Chapter Eighteen

Smoke clogged his throat and burned his eyes. Travis kept low and pulled his shirt over his mouth and nose, but there was no avoiding it.

And Tilda was up here while the building burned around her.

There was a strange quiver in his limbs, one he almost didn't recognize. Fear. He'd thought that reaction had been trained out of him, but the moment he'd learned Tilda was in the building it had settled low in his gut and wouldn't leave until he had the girl in his arms.

He tested the knob to Willow's apartment. It was warm but not hot. It also wouldn't turn. "Stand to the side," he told Jake. After his friend was out of the way of any potential backdraft, Travis kicked the door with the heel of his boot. With a snap of wood, it burst inward.

"Tilda!" He wiped his eyes and scanned the living room.

Jake ran for the kitchen as Travis headed down the short hall. He checked Tilda's room first. She wasn't there, not in the closet or under the bed.

"Here!" Jake's shout had Travis springing to his feet. He raced into the hallway as fire streaked a long trail along the ceiling over his head.

Jake stepped from the bathroom carrying a mound covered in sopping towels. Only the two legs hanging beneath his arm identified it as human.

"Tilda." He lifted one of the towels to see two big brown eyes open wide in fright. All of his muscles went slack, and he had to brace his hand against the wall. She was all right. For now, at least.

She coughed and held her arms out to him.

Travis took her from his friend. Her small weight settled on his hip,. Holding this little girl, protecting her, felt all kinds of right in a way he never would have imagined. Pressing the edge of one of the towels to her face, he ran for the door, Jake a step behind. They took the stairs in record time and burst from the building.

Travis sucked oxygen into his lungs as he made for Willow.

She screamed for her daughter, and Chris, seeing them, all but shoved Willow out of his arms. As soon as her feet hit the ground, she sprinted forward. She ran her hands over her daughter, looking for any injury.

Tilda reached for her, like she had to Travis, and he passed her over to her mom, stripping the towels from her as he did.

Tilda wrapped her arms and legs around Willow, burying her face in the crook of her mother's neck.

Travis stepped close and wrapped his arms around the both of them. Jesus, that could have gone so much worse. He eyed the building. Two fire trucks had pulled up and the firefighters were busy setting up the hoses, but the building was a lost cause. The fire was burning hot and fast, and Willow would be lucky to salvage any of her property.

Willow's shoulders shook, and he tightened his arms. Thank fuck Willow had been giving him the cold shoulder all week. He'd been determined to see her and set things right. It was the reason his friends had decided to have dinner in Swansboro, thinking she might be more receptive to a group activity and they were trying to be his wingmen. And it was the reason he had decided to drive straight to her shop instead of the restaurant. He had taken a separate vehicle from his friends, but when they'd seen the smoke upon entering the town, they'd all hightailed it over here as quickly as they safely could.

"She okay?" Chris asked.

"Yeah." Travis hadn't seen any burns on Tilda, though he wanted her to get checked out more thoroughly. She had a small cough, but for being trapped in a burning building, she seemed to be doing well.

He looked up and got his first good look at his friend. Chris's bottom lip was starting to swell. Angry red scratches ran up and down his forearms and one marred his cheek, dangerously close to his left eye. "What...?"

Chris nodded at Willow. "Next time, I'm going into the burning building. I'd rather face an ambush with fifty hostiles than hold onto that wildcat again."

Sam wrapped her arm around Chris's waist. "Jesus, that was intense."

Caroline stepped up next to Willow and held up a bottle of water. "Why don't you try to get Tilda to drink a little of this?"

Willow swiped her fingers over her cheek and nodded. She pulled away from Travis and held the bottle to Tilda's mouth, helping her drink.

Willow held her body stiffly, and Travis didn't like the haggard expression on her face, the hollowness of her eyes. "Hey, Tilda's safe," he said. "Everything is going to be okay."

She barked out a bitter laugh. "What about this is okay?"

Travis reached for her shoulder, but she stepped away.

"What happened?" Jake asked.

"That's what I'd like to know." Fire Marshal Williams planted himself next to Willow, his thumbs hooked in his belt. "It hasn't even been a week, Miz Janna. What did you do now?"

Willow's face went red. "I didn't do anything. I wasn't here."

The fire marshal's eyebrows shot up. "But your daughter was? Alone?"

Tilda burrowed deeper into her mom's embrace, her chin quivering.

"Hey." Travis tried to make his voice light, but it came out a low growl. "They've just been through a traumatic experience. Now is not the time."

Willow and the fire marshal ignored him.

"She was supposed to go down to the shop to be with Mandi." Willow rubbed Tilda's back. "What did you do when I was gone, baby? Did you play with anything you shouldn't have? Try to cook yourself something?"

Tilda shook her head. "I wanted to finish my book. When I smelled smoke, I soaked towels like the fireman in school told us to."

Travis pointed at the building. "The fire didn't start in the apartment. When we went up to get Tilda it was just smoke in the apartment, no fire."

Williams gave a little harumph. "So you left something on the stove that caught fire."

"No." Mandi joined them, her eyebrows drawing together. "We stopped cooking at noon. There was nothing on in the kitchen."

"So what happened?" Williams asked.

Mandi shook her head. "I don't know. I was in the front of the shop and suddenly it felt like fire was all around me." A tear ran down her cheek, and she brushed it away. "Thank God Tilda's all right." She leaned forward and kissed the girl's head.

"Well, something happened to start the fire." Williams hefted his belt. "When I find out what, I'm going to make sure you'll never be able to open your business in Swansboro again. And when your insurance company finds out how negligent you've been, good luck getting paid."

Willow staggered back. Sam and Caroline gathered around her, lending their support.

The back of Travis's neck went hot. He stepped into the marshal's space. "You can fuck right off." Jake laid a hand on his shoulder, but he shrugged it off. "A woman almost lost her child, just lost her home, her business, and you come in here with that attitude? Go to hell."

Chris pulled Travis back a step, and Jake smoothly slid in between him and the marshal. "Understandably," Jake said, "emotions are running high. After your team finds the source of the fire, you'll let us know."

"Now you're giving me orders?" The marshal's eyebrows shot up.

"Not an order." Jake crossed his arms. "Just an expectation that you'll do your job."

Travis had had enough. He turned his back on the man and strode to Willow. "Ignore him. He's an ass—" He looked at Tilda. "He's a jerk." He cupped Willow's cheek and swiped his thumb over the mascara that had pooled beneath her eyes.

She didn't lean into his touch like usual. "I'm going to take Tilda to the hospital. I want to make sure she doesn't have any lung issues."

"Of course. I'll drive—"

"The ambulance is pulling up now." Willow nodded down the street.

"Okay. I'll follow you and meet you there."

"Don't bother." She hefted Tilda higher on her hip. "I don't want you there."

All the oxygen was sucked from his lungs. "What? Why?"

She stared him down, her eyes hard. "You kept me away from Tilda. Prevented me from going to her when she needed me most. I won't forget that."

His mouth fell open. "I was protecting you. And I was the better choice to go in after Tilda."

"I am her *mother*." Willow jabbed a finger at his face. "What you did was unforgiveable."

"Willow...."

She turned and walked to the approaching medics. "She was in the smoke for I don't know how long."

Travis made to follow her, but Caroline grabbed his arm. "Let her be for now. There is no arguing with that level of rage."

"But it doesn't make sense."

"Women aren't supposed to make sense," Chris said.

Sam slapped the back of his head before turning to Travis. "I get why you did it, but I understand why she's pissed. If someone tried to get between me and Maddie when she needed my help, I'd go ballistic, too."

"We're trained in rescues." Travis shook his head. This was bullshit. The stress of the day was clouding Willow's mind. He started for the ambulance, and was stopped by his friends again.

"We'll go to the hospital and see if she'll let us help her." Jake nudged him toward his Jeep. "And I'll call if she wants to see you. But the best thing you can do right now is go home and wait for her to cool off."

Travis gripped his hips. He didn't want to listen to Jake, but the man made sense. Besides, he couldn't take it if she kept looking at him the way she just had. Like he was dirt beneath her heels. He clenched his hands, focused on his breathing, and nodded. Willow would calm down. She'd realize he'd done what was best.

Willow and Tilda climbed in the back of the ambulance and the doors shut. The truck pulled away, lights flashing but without its siren.

Travis swallowed. Tilda would probably have liked to hear the siren. The ambulance got smaller as it drove down the street, diminishing, just like his hopes and expectations. He told himself that Willow would come to her senses, but he'd never seen her so angry.

And he couldn't help thinking that his future had gone up in flames, just like her building.

Chapter Nineteen

WILLOW IGNORED THE RECEPTIONIST squawking behind her and stormed into Calhoun's office. She slammed the door behind her.

Calhoun started, a tuft of platinum hair straying down his forehead with the movement. "Willow? What are you doing here?" He offered her a sad smile. "I heard about your fire. It's a damned shame."

She stomped to his desk and planted her palms on the surface. "Is it? Or is it exactly what you wanted to happen?"

His bushy eyebrows drew together. "What are you talking about?"

"The fire." She smacked her hand down, and the pencil on the desk jumped. "Did you start it?"

Calhoun gaped. "Start it? I would never...."

"You clogged my toilet. You seem perfectly happy intentionally causing property damage." Every muscle in Willow's body trembled. She'd been running on adrenaline and anger for the past twenty-four hours.

"There's a big difference between clogging a toilet and setting a fire." His eyes rounded in outrage. "Someone could have been hurt."

Willow reached behind her, fumbling for his guest chair. She grabbed the arms and slumped into it, spent. The backs of her eyes burned, and she closed them so he wouldn't see the sheen of tears.

She believed him. Calhoun had been the only target she knew to direct her accusations, her wrath, and now she had nothing.

Willow dug her nails into her palm. A spike of longing shot through her, a need to be wrapped in Travis's arms so great it stole her breath.

She shouldn't want him. His betrayal had been too great. But her body didn't understand that. Her body wanted to be pressed against his, letting his strength seep into her as he held her tight. Calling him now would be a surrender, a concession that she accepted his actions, which she didn't think she ever could.

How often would Tilda be in danger like that? the part of her that wanted Travis desperately asked. The situation was likely to never happen again, but she just couldn't let it go. Tilda had needed her, and Travis had forcibly kept her from her daughter.

A chair squeaked. Fabric rustled. Calhoun circled his desk and sat in the guest chair next to hers. "I talked to my wife about you." He huffed out a chuckle. "Or more accurately, she talked to me about you."

Willow opened her eyes, frowning. "I thought your wife...."

"Had passed?" He nodded. "Four years ago. I still like to go to the cemetery and tell her about my day. You know how it is."

Not really. When Bill had died, she hadn't once felt the urge to talk with him. She'd mourned him, mourned everything he and Tilda had lost, and moved on. But theirs hadn't been a great love. Not like her and—

She cut that absurd thought off. "What did you talk about?"

Calhoun laced his fingers together and rested his hands on his softly-rounded belly. "She wasn't happy with my little prank. Thought it was most ungentlemanly of me." He sniffed. "I'm supposed to tell you, well, I'm sorry."

Willow would have smiled if she'd had the energy. He looked and sounded like a scolded child. "Accepted."

"Really?" His eyebrows arched.

She sighed. "I have enough problems without keeping you on the roster."

He turned toward her, leaning on the armrest. "I didn't cause the fire."

She nodded. "I believe you." Maybe it had been faulty wiring. An ember from someone's fire pit that blew onto her building. The fire department would find out eventually. Hopefully sooner rather than later. Her insurance company had told her they wouldn't pay out her claim until the cause was known.

And if it was in any way Willow's fault, they wouldn't pay out at all.

"Can you tell your young fella that?" Calhoun asked. "I really don't want a third visit from him."

"He's not my fellow." Not anymore. Her chest tightened. She couldn't forget the look in his eyes when she'd told him to stay away yesterday. The disbelief. The betrayal. And for the first time since they'd met, he'd actually listened to her and kept his distance. She'd expected him to come to the hospital anyway, had prepared herself for the fight.

She should have been happy when he hadn't shown. Instead, all she'd felt was empty.

Calhoun frowned. "Are you sure about that? Because the last time I saw that boy he made it very clear that you were his. That level of feeling doesn't just go away."

Willow rubbed her forehead. "I ended it. He...did something I can't forgive." She didn't elaborate. Even in her pissed-off state, she knew that no one would understand that Travis keeping her out of the fire while he saved her daughter was a good enough reason to end their relationship. If it hadn't happened to her, she wouldn't understand it.

But it had happened to her, and she was still furious. "I don't have time for him, anyway. There's work and there's Tilda. That fills up my day."

His pale blue eyes gazed at her steadily. "I'm going to give you some advice you don't want to hear, but that's when advice is most needed. Your business is not as important as your relationships, not even close. When I think about all the time I spent at this office when I could have been home with my Adeline or taking her out to lunch, well, it breaks my heart."

Willow pressed her lips flat. "You weren't a single parent. I have to work hard to provide for her."

"There's always a reason." Calhoun's lips quirked up. "Putting work above people is a bad habit. I'm too old to break it, but there's hope for you."

She blew out a breath and sank deeper into the chair. Calhoun was right; she didn't want to hear it. Mainly because she knew it was true. She'd been working so hard to give Tilda everything she needed, everything except her time and attention.

But she didn't see a way out. Now that her business had burned, she would have to work twice as hard to rebuild. She didn't even want to think about all the paperwork, the permits, the state forms she'd need to file in order to get back open.

Do I have to rebuild?

She pushed that thought away. What else was she to do? She made jam. She created new recipes. She was good at it. She loved that part of it. She'd just have to deal with all the business crap that came with it.

"I'd better be going." Willow toyed with the hem of her new-to-her T-shirt. She and Tilda had hit the thrift stores that morning for some clothes. There hadn't been any cute forties-style dresses, so Willow was stuck in jeans and tees for the foreseeable future. Instead of sleeping in their cute apartment last night, they'd stayed at a charmless motel. It was like Willow had lost her identity along with her business.

She rubbed her breastbone. She really should get up and get moving. She had a to-do list a mile long. But she didn't want to move. She knew the next step she should take, but didn't know if it was the one she wanted to take.

Her body was numb as she stood. She knew the path to recreate *It's Your Jam*. It was familiar. She'd trod it before. And she'd do again. What else was there to do?

"Thanks," she said. "And I'm sorry for accusing you of setting the fire."

He rose and walked her to his door. "Not at all. I'm glad we got that all sorted." He rested his hand on the doorknob. "You know, this could be the perfect opportunity for you. I'm still interested in purchasing your property, at a discounted price now, of course. Why don't you think about if the hassle of going through a rebuild is worth it to you. Give me a call when you make a decision."

Willow blinked. Unbelievable. Her property had just burned and he was still trying to wheedle a deal. She wondered what his Adeline would have to say about that.

She shook her head and tramped from his office.

Chapter Twenty

"How long is this going to take?" Travis pressed his palm on the desk and leaned over Ryan's shoulder.

"I started two minutes ago." Ryan's fingers flew over his keyboard. "Back off, would you?"

Travis huffed a breath but did as his friend said. He paced the blue carpet in Ryan's combo home office and game room, feeling as agitated as a caged cat with every step. Willow was out there, alone but for Tilda, dealing with the loss of her business, her home. There was a sick feeling in his gut that warned him this fire wasn't an accident, and he wanted nothing more than to be by her side, helping her, protecting her.

And she didn't want him.

"This company actually has decent firewalls." Ryan frowned. "It might take a bit. Why aren't we just telling the fire marshal and cops about Willow's cameras? I'm sure they're as eager to know the cause of the fire as you."

"It will take too long." Travis ran his hand up the back of his head. "If there's something on the video, I want to know now." Or if there was someone. After his last conversation with Calhoun, he didn't think the man would have done something like this, but Travis needed to be sure. If someone had intentionally set the fire, he was getting Willow somewhere safe, no matter what she said.

Ryan sighed. "You do know this is illegal, right? I'm risking a lot for a woman who Chris says wants nothing to do with you."

Travis clenched his hands. Chris didn't know what the fuck he was talking about. Yes, Willow had told Travis she didn't want to see him anymore. Had looked through him like he was nothing. But she'd been scared. Angry. She'd come around.

His legs went weak, and he crumpled onto the small sofa next to Ryan's desk. He pressed his fingers into his temples. What if she'd meant it? What if the woman he loved wanted nothing to do with him?

Ryan spun in his chair, raising his eyebrows. "Well? Is this woman worth the risk?"

"You're the only person I know who can do this." Ryan was the unofficial hacker of their group. He was trained in advanced communications, and when it came to computer skills, he ran rings around anyone else Travis knew. "I hate to put you at risk—"

Ryan waved his hand, dismissing that. "You know I have your back. What's a little jail time between friends? But I ask again, is she worth it? How are you going to feel if we do all this and Suzy Homemaker sets up shop with someone else?"

Travis's skin flushed hot, then went clammy. He couldn't even wrap his brain around Willow with another man. From the moment he'd seen her, he'd known she was his. He'd felt it, bone-deep.

But life didn't always play fair. He knew that better than most. Sometimes a bomb took out an innocent. Or an illness struck down a child.

And sometimes, the man didn't get the woman.

He met his friend's eyes and swallowed. "Even if she won't have me, I need to make sure she's safe."

Ryan narrowed his eyes. "It's like that, is it?"

"Yeah." He nodded. "It's like that."

Ryan held his gaze a moment longer before turning back to his computer. "Christ, I'm going to be the last man standing soon. Viper sees you and Psych and Trip all partnered up, and he's getting all soft and squishy inside. Mark my words, he'll be next. I'm going to be surrounded by couples and babies in no time." His tone made it sound like he'd rather be swimming with piranhas.

Travis smiled weakly. "You'll get to be the fun uncle." Of all his friends, Ryan was the one who Travis had the hardest time picturing with a family of his own. An uncle might be the closest he got to having kids.

Ryan's fingers paused over the keyboard. He cocked his head. "Uncle. Yeah, I can do that." He waved Travis over. "I can also get you the access you need, because I fucking rock."

Travis stood and strode to the desk. Willow's account with the security company was open on the screen, listing each of her cameras. "Let's go through them, one by one, starting yesterday at the time of the fire and working backwards."

Ryan hit the link for camera one, set the date and time filters, and hit play. It caught the large crowd of people on the street, staring in horror at Willow's building. Ryan used his mouse to move the timestamp backwards, watching the video in reverse. Nothing suspicious.

Camera two captured the hallway in Willow's shop. It showed smoke at the beginning, but no one was visible except for Mandi walking to the bathroom an hour earlier. Cameras three and four were busts, as well.

Camera five showed the alley in back of the kitchen. Ryan had to rewind several minutes before any video was recoverable. "The fire started here," Ryan said. "Knocked out this camera first."

Travis only nodded. His eyes were focused on the screen.

And the figure in a dark hoodie by Willow's kitchen door. "Go back ten minutes. Let's watch this from the beginning."

"Yep." Ryan jumped the feed back in time. He sped it up in five second increments until there was movement.

"Son of a bitch." The same figure appeared on the screen. They watched as it splashed the back wall of the building with liquid from a gasoline can. The man, for Travis could tell by his movements and build the figure was male, slid off his backpack and removed what looked like piles of rags. He stuffed them under the crease of the door, and dumped accelerant on them, too. Then he stood back, lit a match, and dropped it onto the pile.

Travis's feet moved before he even realized it. "Send that footage to the fire marshal and the Swansboro PD," he called back to Ryan. He pulled his phone from his pocket as he made his way out of Ryan's apartment and to his Jeep.

"Pick up," he muttered as the line rang. It took him by surprise when Willow actually did.

"Travis." Her voice caught. "I don't have time for this."

She didn't have time for him.

Too bad.

"The fire at your store was arson," he said with no lead up. He jumped in his vehicle and turned the ignition. "And it wasn't Calhoun." He hadn't been able to see the face in the video, but the figure had been much too young and slender for the property developer.

"I know it wasn't Calhoun," she said. "But how do you know it was arson?"

"I pulled up the video footage from your cameras." He pulled onto the highway heading to Swansboro.

"The cameras." She groaned. "I forgot about those."

"How did you know Calhoun wasn't involved?"

"I went to talk to him. He told me he didn't do it, and I believe him."

His knuckles went white around the steering wheel. "You went to speak to a man you suspected of burning your building?" he gritted out. He and Willow were going to have a talk about risk assessment.

She ignored his question. "What now? Do I go to the police?"

"Ryan is taking care of that." He flicked on his turn signal and merged into the fast lane. "Right now you need to pack up whatever you and Tilda have and get ready for me to pick you up."

She hesitated. "I don't think that's necessary."

"This isn't up for negotiation. This goes beyond you being mad at me." His speedometer edged up. "This is about you and Tilda being safe. Are you at your motel?" Jake had told him where he'd dropped them off after Tilda had been released from the hospital. Travis had needed that thread of connection.

"Do you really think we're in danger?" she asked in a small voice.

Travis exhaled. "Someone wants to hurt you, but I'm not going to let that happen. I need you somewhere I can control, where you'll be safe. You and Tilda will stay with me until this gets sorted." He could set her up in another hotel under a fake name, but he'd be on edge every moment they were apart. "Please, sweetness."

She was silent a moment. "Okay. I'll pack. It won't take long."

His shoulders inched away from his ears. "Thank you." He lightened his voice. "It won't be so bad. You can use my kitchen, sell your jams online until you get your shop sorted."

"That would be nice, thanks." She said something to Tilda, the sound muffled over the line, before coming back on. "Okay, we'll see you soon."

"Soon." He cut the call. He was getting close to Swansboro, but was still too far for his liking. He wouldn't be easy until Willow and Tilda were safe with him.

He stomped on the gas pedal. He was going to get his girls.

Chapter Twenty-One

WILLOW HAD INSISTED ON following Travis in her own car the other day when Travis had come to pick her and Tilda up, but now she almost regretted it. She gave her passenger the side-eye, hoping most of the crumbs were contained to his body but knowing they weren't. She would need to vacuum.

"These are great. I haven't had them in forever." Tony poured another handful of goldfish crackers into his palm and tossed them in his mouth.

She'd assumed when she'd bought the extra-large carton of crackers that they'd last Tilda months. She'd assumed wrong.

Tony was her babysitter for the afternoon. He didn't seem to have the same restraint when it came to snacks and sweets as Travis did. Eating Tilda's snacks at least seemed to distract him from the fact he wasn't in the driver's seat. He'd grumped about being relegated to passenger, but Willow didn't care. He could mumble about defensive driving all he wanted. It was her car, and she was going to be behind the wheel. The way her life was spinning about like one of Tilda's marbles, Willow needed at least that small bit of control.

"When is Travis getting off work?" She pulled into the long line of cars waiting to pick-up students at the elementary school.

"His appointment with the base doc should be over by now." Tony tilted his head to see the beginning of the long line, his chocolate brown hair falling over his forehead. "There's gotta be a better way to organize this," he muttered.

She frowned. "I thought he was cleared for duty already."

"He was, but with a bullet wound they just like to check in to make sure everything is going as it should since he's back on active."

She winced. A bullet wound. She still couldn't believe Travis had been shot. Thank God it had happened before she'd met him. She didn't know how she would handle getting that news.

It was a moot point now. She rubbed her breastbone. She'd made it clear that just because she and Tilda were staying with him didn't mean she wanted to restart their relationship. She'd even managed to make it sound believable.

"Hey," Tony said, his dark eyes sympathetic, "Travis getting shot was a rare event. We have very few injuries. You don't have to worry."

She smiled brightly. "I wasn't worried."

"Uh huh."

She gripped the wheel as her car crawled forward. Even if she wasn't in a relationship with Travis, she feared she'd always worry about him. And she would never know if anything had happened to him, of if he'd separated from the Marines and gotten a job as a parachuting instructor, or if he'd married and had five kids and three dogs on a farm somewhere.

Her breath was sucked from her lungs. It would be better if she didn't know about that last one.

"There she is." Tony lowered his window and waved to Tilda. "Hey, girl. How was school?" he asked as she climbed into her seat in the back.

"Fun." She hooked herself in. "Me and some other kids took a bus to a special class at another school. A real astronaut talked to us about space, and we had to pretend we were trapped on the moon and figure a way off, and we even got to eat their ice cream!" She wrinkled her nose. "It was dry and weird."

Willow pulled onto the street. She'd forgotten Tilda was going to be included in this week's gifted program, even before she'd tested. Principal Harker had wanted to see how Tilda managed it. She would have to remember to thank the man.

"That's great," Willow said. "Now mind your manners and say hello to Tony. You remember him, don't you?"

"He's Viper." She drummed her feet against the front seats. "Hi, Viper."

Willow reached back and stilled Tilda's kicking. "She loved that all you guys had nicknames," she told Tony. Although Travis had only told Tilda about one of his. He'd confessed to Willow he had no idea how to explain One Shot to a little girl. "How'd you get yours?" she asked.

Tony shifted. "It's, uh, a long story."

He sounded embarrassed. She arched an eyebrow. Which meant it was probably a good story. Before she left Travis's house, she was determined to hear it.

"Did you get my fish?" Tilda asked from the back.

"Yes, I got your crackers." Her lips twitched as Tony silently slid the carton to a spot by his feet. "I also got the makings for homemade mac and cheese and ice cream for tonight. Real ice cream."

Tilda cheered, and Willow echoed the sentiment. It had been a hard couple of days, and they needed comfort food.

Tilda related everything the astronaut had said and done as they drove to Jacksonville. By the time they rolled up to Travis's townhouse, Willow felt ready to launch into space.

Travis's Jeep Commander was in the driveway. Travis had insisted that Willow park her car in the garage. She pressed the button to open the garage door. "Will you stay for dinner?" she asked Tony. "There will be plenty of food." And with Tony there, she and Travis had less chances for uncomfortable conversations.

"No, thanks. I already have plans." He grabbed several grocery bags and walked her and Tilda to the door and herded them inside.

Travis met them in the kitchen. "Thanks, man." He took a bag and set it on the counter. "I've got it from here."

Tony nodded, said goodbye, and sauntered out the front door.

Willow narrowed her eyes. It all felt very much like a hand-off, with her and Tilda as the ball or suitcase or whatever the hell got handed off.

She set about putting the groceries away. When it came to Tilda's safety, she could feel like an object for a couple of days.

"Did you have a good day?" Willow didn't know who Travis was asking, but Tilda jumped to answer, telling him all about the astronaut's talk. When she finally came up for breath, Travis said, "Well, I don't think I can top astronaut ice cream, but I got you a little something, Tilda."

He reached for a bag with the name of a toy store printed on it and pulled out a new puzzle and a small cloth sack. "They didn't have any unicorn ones, but there were some other nice animals."

"Marbles!" Tilda squealed when she opened the sack. "Thank you."

"Not in here," Willow said as Tilda started to pull them out. "I don't need to slip on one when I'm boiling cheese."

Tilda ran from the room.

"Boiling cheese?" Travis poked among the items she'd left on the counter. "What are you making?"

"Mac and cheese." She pointed at a head of lettuce. "There's also some salad makings if you want to get that started."

They each turned to their tasks, an awkward silence filling the room.

"Everything go okay at the doctor's?" she finally asked.

"Everything's fine." He chopped a tomato into neat chunks.

Willow made a roux then slowly added cream. The back of her neck itched. "Uh, thanks for getting Tilda the marbles and puzzle. That was sweet."

"No problem. She deserves a treat." He rubbed the back of his neck. "Christ, the kid lost everything. She deserves a hell of a lot more."

She took a deep breath, her chest expanding. He really was a good man. He'd made a mistake the day of the fire, but that didn't change his essence.

"Do many girls her age like marbles?" he asked. He turned from the sink where he was rinsing the lettuce. "Not to sound sexist, but marbles seem more like a boy thing."

Willow stared at the bubbles slowing rising to the surface of the sauce. "Her father collected them since he was a young boy. I think having the same hobby as him makes her feel connected." And connections were important. Was she wrong to try to sever the one between her and Travis?

She didn't need to think about that now. She cleared her throat. "The fire marshal said I can go to my building tomorrow and see if I can find anything to salvage. Maybe not everything is lost."

Travis set the bowl of salad aside. "I'll go with you."

She shook her head. "You're busy. I'm sure I can find someone else—"

"No." He stepped close to the stove. To her. "Picking through the ruins of your life will be tough. I'm going to be there with you."

The back of her throat burned. "Thanks." She added the shredded cheese and watched the mixture bubble. "I never thanked you. For that night. For getting Tilda. I know it was a mistake restraining me, but you still went into a burning building to save my daughter. I should have thanked you."

He gripped her shoulders and turned her to face him. "You don't have to thank me. And it wasn't a mistake."

Her eyebrows snapped together. "What? You mean you still think you were right to stop me from getting to Tilda?"

"I was right." His fingers dug into her skin as she tried to step back. "If you're alone, of course you'll do whatever you have to for Tilda. But if I'm there, you won't take foolish risks."

She ground her jaw. She'd thought there could be compromise, but there wasn't with Travis. It was all or nothing.

She ripped from his grip and turned back to the stove. She didn't have all to give him. If Travis thought he was right to stand between her and Tilda in some instances, what other things would he try to get between?

No one could come between her and her daughter. It had been just the two of them for so long now. Her lungs squeezed. She wouldn't let a man come between that. Between them.

Even if he meant well.

Even if she loved him.

Chapter Twenty-Two

THE ACRID SCENT OF burnt wood and metal still hung in the air. Travis left a real estate agents office and headed to the next business down the street from *It's Your Jam*.

At least, it had been Willow's jam. It had been her life. Poking through the rubble with her yesterday had been heartbreaking. She'd tried to keep her emotions in check, but he could see how devastating it had been seeing the ruins of her home, her business.

The asshole who'd done this to her was going to pay. He jerked open the glass front door to a retro record store, the walls covered with vinyl albums. First Travis would find the arsonist, make sure he went away for a long time, and then he'd work on repairing his and Willow's relationship. He'd had a devil of a time breaking through her walls when they'd first met. He could do it again.

Even though this new wall seemed to be twice as high and reinforced with concrete.

A middle-aged woman with streaks of green in her dark hair greeted him from behind the counter. "How can I help you today?"

Travis opened his manilla folder and took out a photo Ryan had pulled from the camera at the rear of Willow's shop. "I was hoping you might recognize this man." He laid the eight by ten glossy on the counter. "I know you can't see his face, but does anything about his build or what he's wearing seem familiar?"

The woman picked a pair of glasses up from next to the register and set them on her nose. She frowned. "No, I can't say that I recognize him. Is this the man who torched the jam shop?"

Travis rubbed his temple. His headache had started three businesses ago when he'd heard the same answer repeated over and over. No one recognized the man in the photo. Travis hadn't expected them to, not really, but it was still frustrating.

He ignored her question and pulled out another photo. "Did you happen to notice this man in the neighborhood the day of the fire?"

She took the picture of Calhoun. Shook her head. "Can't say I did. But unless he came into my shop, the chances of me seeing anyone are slim to none. I don't peer outside much." She quirked her mouth when she passed the photo back. "Although when I was washing my windows, I did see that guy who works in the jam shop. He used to come in here frequently when he'd get off work, but I hadn't seen him for weeks."

His shoulder blades drew together. "That was the day of the fire?"

"Yep." The bell above the door rang, and the woman waved at the newcomer. "I know because I remember thinking I wished I'd waited one more day to wash the windows. The fire blew a lot of soot and gunk over here, and I had to wash them again."

"Did you talk to the guy when you saw him?"

Her eyebrows drew together. "No. He was down the street. In fact, I remember thinking it was odd he'd parked so far away. You...you don't think he could have anything to do with the fire, do you?"

Travis held up the first photo again. "Is he the same build as the guy in this picture? Could it be the same person?"

"Yeess?" She drew the word out, disbelieving. "I guess it could be him. But why would he—"

"Thank you." Travis resisted the urge to lean over the counter and kiss the woman. "You don't know how helpful you've been." He gathered his photos and hurried from the store. When he hit the sidewalk, he pulled out his phone and called Ryan.

"Yo," the other man answered.

"I need you to check out a name." He blinked, then swore. "I don't know the last name. First name Ben, in his twenties, worked for Willow until she fired him a couple weeks ago. Can you find him, or should I call Willow for his last name?"

The sound of a keyboard clacking was his only answer. "Got him. Ben Giles. A simple search of Ben and *It's Your Jam* brought it up. Whoa."

Travis paced toward his Jeep. "Whoa what?"

"I think this is your guy," Ryan said.

"How can you know that already? How did you hack into anything that fast?"

"I didn't." Ryan sucked in a sharp breath. "I'm just on his socials, and this dude sounds like a psychopath. An angry one. Especially at, and I'm quoting here, 'the bitch who fired' him."

Travis's pulse pounded in his ears. "I want everything you can get on him. His address, current employer, anything. If he has a phone, I want it tracked."

"And send this info onto the PD?"

Travis hesitated for only a second. A part of him wanted to take care of this himself, and the police would only get in the way of that. But the smarter, more rational part of him didn't want to face the possibility of jail time when the cops could get Giles off the street just as well. "Anything that won't get you in trouble."

He cut the call and climbed into his vehicle. He'd go home, set up surveillance on the asshole until the police arrested him. They had nothing but suspicions right now, but Travis didn't doubt that with a small amount of investigation the truth would out. The one time he had met Ben, the guy didn't strike Travis as a mastermind, criminal or otherwise.

His phone rang as he pulled onto the street. He answered without looking at the display. "Kowalski here."

"I just got to your place." Chris's voice was tight. "I was bringing Willow some lunch before my shift to watch her."

"And? What's wrong?" His foot went heavy on the gas pedal.

"Your house is empty, man. Your girl's not here."

Chapter Twenty-Three

"Dammit." Willow gave up on the charger and put her hand back on the steering wheel. She would need to buy a new one, and fast if she wanted to use her phone tomorrow. Maybe the drug store would have one.

She exited the highway and drove into Swansboro. The school administrator had said something about an upset stomach before the connection had cut away. She didn't know what Travis kept in his house in the way of medicine, but she'd better stop and get some after she picked Tilda up.

Willow rolled her neck. And the day had been going so well before the call. In Travis's kitchen she'd created a new recipe, a strawberry mojito preserves, that tasted pretty darn fantastic, if she did say so herself. A chain of boutique hotels based in the South had contacted her about supplying them with her jams to serve with their breakfasts. They wanted to give their guests as many local products as possible, and who was she to argue? She'd only need to rent a commercial kitchen for a few hours a day. She could make enough jam to sell just online to pay the bills. A weight had lifted off her chest when she'd run the numbers.

But now her girl was sick. That was enough to ruin any mother's day.

Her phone rang, Travis's name lighting up the screen. She put it on speaker then tried to hold the charging cord at exactly the right angle to keep her phone alive. "Hi," she said. "What's up?"

"Where are you?" His voice was a rough growl. A shiver danced down her spine. It shouldn't have been sexy, him taking that tone with her, but it was.

"Heading to Tilda's school. I have to pick her up. She's sick."

"I'll meet you there," he said. "Wait for me."

Willow lifted her hand to put her turn signal on. "What? Why? I'll be back at your place in a little bit." After she stopped at the drug store.

"You shouldn't have gone alone." A horn blared on his end, and he cursed. "You're not safe," he gritted out.

She pressed her lips together. "I'm just heading to the school. It's public, and no one knows where I'm going anyways. It's fine." She'd made a point of checking if anyone had followed her from Travis's place. There hadn't been any cars behind her until she hit the busier streets. She *was* being cautious.

"I'll meet you there," he repeated. "Willow, I know who torched your building."

She waited. Blinked. "And? Don't keep me in suspense. Who did it?"

There was no answer. She looked down at her phone and groaned. The screen was dark. She wiggled the charging cord, but nothing happened. Her phone was good and dead.

She turned into the parking lot of the elementary school. She'd have to wait for Travis now, not if she didn't want him coming all the way here only to turn around when he found her gone. She needed to memorize his number instead of relying on her phone's contact information. She had no way to reach him without her cell phone, and that bothered her. Maybe someone in the office had a charger she could use.

She parked, but stayed inside her car a moment longer, gripping the steering wheel. He knew who the arsonist was. Her nightmare was over. She didn't think she could stay in his townhouse much longer. It was too hard being around him so much, sitting next to him on the sofa and fighting over the remote, seeing him play with Tilda. Every second they were alone together, it wasn't only Travis she was fighting, but she was fighting herself, as well.

Something inside her wouldn't let her move forward with Travis. And if she couldn't move forward, she needed to back the hell away or else she'd break. It was like there was a locked door between them. A part of her needed to find that key, go through, because she loved him like she'd never loved another man.

Another part of her didn't even want to look for the key. She stared at the school. For the past five years it had been her and Tilda against the world. If she let someone else in.... Well, she didn't know what would happen, but it had the potential to be very bad.

Or very, very good.

She blew out a shuddering breath. She was scared. She needed to admit that to herself. Her reluctance had nothing to do with Travis keeping her from Tilda during the fire. He'd pissed her off, but she could move past that. His actions were a handy excuse to keep her heart safe.

Her gut churned. She didn't like being a coward. She grabbed her purse, shoved her useless phone inside, and climbed from her car. But she didn't know if she could talk herself into bravery.

She strode across the parking lot. A homeless man in cut-off jeans and a hooded-sweatshirt that looked like it hadn't seen a washing machine in years loitered by the steps. She was tempted to change her route, walk up the handicap ramp to avoid him, but told herself she was being judgy and stupid. She wasn't looking her best either, in yet another pair of used jeans and sneakers. She needed to start buying some dresses and heels to feel like herself again.

Her foot hit the first step when the man looked up into her face. She froze. "Ben?"

"Took you long enough to get to your sick kid, but it doesn't surprise me you don't give a shit about her." He shoved his hand into his hoodie's pocket. "You don't care about anyone but yourself."

She faltered back a step. "I came from Jacksonville." Her pulse kicked up. "How do you know Tilda's sick?"

He dropped his voice an octave, sounding like a much older man. "Mrs. Janna? Your daughter is with the school nurse with an upset stomach. It would be best if you come down and get her."

She fell back another step. Ben had been the one to call her about Tilda. Dots starting connecting all over. She'd lay money Travis had been about to tell her Ben had been the one to set fire to her place, too.

"Why?" she whispered. Yes, she'd fired him, but it was just a minimum wage job. No one committed a felony over a minimum wage job.

He pulled his hand from his pocket, his knuckles white around the handle of a knife. The blade had to be at least eight inches long. It glinted in the sun.

A vise clamped around her lungs. She should run, but she didn't hold out much hope that she'd outpace him. He was young and lean and she had a hate-hate relationship with exercise.

Ben took a step toward her, his chest heaving.

Her purse slid off her shoulder, and she gripped the strap. She had some vague thought she could swing it around like a soft, lumpy mace, use it as some kind of weapon. The reality was she knew she was screwed.

Everything she'd miss in this life darted through her head. Watching Tilda grow. Seeing the woman she'd become. Making more babies with the man she loved.

The backs of her eyes burned. She'd been embarrassed that she'd judged a man who'd looked disheveled, out of place, and had gotten too close. And now he had a knife, while she only had regrets.

She should have listened to her instincts.

Chapter Twenty-Four

TRAVIS GUNNED IT INTO the parking lot. He spotted Willow at once, her hands held up in front of her as she backed away from her ex-employee. Large cement planters lined the walkway to the school, blocking the way. The fucker was lucky. If they hadn't been there, Ben would have become a hood ornament.

He spun his vehicle as close to Willow as he could get and leapt out. He raced forward, planting his body in front of Willow's, reaching behind him to grip her hip.

His breath chain-sawed out of his throat. She was warm. Alive. After Ryan had called and told him the asshole was at the school, Travis hadn't known what he'd find when he got here. He never wanted to go through the last two minutes of his life again.

Ben blinked at him with bloodshot eyes. "The boyfriend. What the fuck are you doing here?"

"I'm here for Willow and Tilda." With his baggy sweatshirt, it was impossible to tell if Ben carried other weapons. "Why don't we talk about what you're doing here?"

Willow wrapped her fingers around his arm. "He has a knife," she whispered. She tried to tug him backward, but he kept his feet planted. This was ending today.

"I see it." It was hard to miss.

"What I'm doing here?" Ben clutched his lank hair with his free hand. "I'm here to show the bitch just what happens when you mess with someone's life." He stepped to the side to put Willow in his eyesight. "You fucked with the wrong person," he screamed.

Travis moved with him. "It was just a job. People get fired all the time. It will be okay." He gritted his teeth. Usually, he was better at talking someone down. Usually, he wanted a peaceful resolution. His fingers dug into Willow's hip. This time he wanted blood.

"Just a job?" Ben waved his arms, the blade flashing in the sunlight. "My probation officer found out I didn't have a job and told the court. My parents kicked me out. Said they couldn't deal with me anymore. And it's all because of her." He stabbed the knife at Willow, and Travis's muscles went hard.

Willow peeked around his shoulder. "Wait. You have a criminal conviction? You didn't list that on your application."

Travis ground his jaw. After this was over, he'd need to teach Willow how to stay focused during an emergency. "Not an important point right now."

She grumbled. "Just saying he's a liar, too."

Ben's eye twitched. "Why couldn't you burn?"

Travis took another step to the side, taking Willow with him. Her former employee was obviously high on something, which made him unpredictable. Travis hated unpredictable when it came to a fight. He probably had a good forty pounds on the kid, but drugs and crazy imbued some with super strength. He couldn't take a chance trying to disarm the man gently, without inflicting damage. He couldn't hold back, not if it risked Willow in any way.

Travis smiled grimly. He was getting his wish. There would be blood. The only drawback was that Willow was here to see it.

A bell rang somewhere in the school. There was no more time to wait. Ben couldn't still be armed if kids came out of the school.

Travis pushed Willow behind one of the hip-high planters then took a step toward Ben. "Willow should have fired you long ago." He took another step, his weight on the balls of his feet. "You're a loser. You blame all your problems on someone else when the truth is you're the problem."

Ben's body vibrated. "Shut up. You don't know what you're talking about."

Travis forced a chuckle. "I see it often enough with the losers who fail out of basic. Mommy and Daddy did everything for you except teach you how to be a man." A child's playful shriek distantly sounded. Travis edged closer.

"What are you doing?" Willow murmured. "Maybe don't piss off the guy with a big knife?"

Travis noted that she was still behind the barrier but didn't respond. "You were too pathetic to hold down a part-time, minimum-wage job and now want to hurt the woman who called you on your shit."

"No." Sweat rolled down Ben's face.

"You're powerless. Impotent. A child who throws a rock through a window in a tantrum." He kept his gaze at the base of the man's throat. Some people liked to watch the eyes, thinking that would indicate what their opponent was about to do. Travis liked to watch the body. A twitch of the shoulders was the best warning. "Did you cut her electrical, too? That was pathetically easy to fix. I mean, you can't even do that right."

Ben yowled. Like an idiot, he raised his knife arm and charged Travis in the position easiest for a weapons' takeaway.

Travis blocked the knife the same time he punched the asshole in the throat. Lightly. He didn't need the kids seeing a corpse on their front steps. As Ben stumbled back, eyes bulging, Travis grabbed his wrist and twisted. The sound of a bone snapping was followed by the knife hitting the ground.

Travis threw him facedown and checked for weapons before letting the guy curl into the fetal position and wail. He gathered up the knife just as two vehicles raced into the parking lot.

"Wow." Willow's hand flew to her chest. She stared at Travis in a daze. "Wow."

Travis stabbed the knife into the dirt next to a purple flower and pulled Willow into his arms. Her heartbeat rabbited against his chest, and he squeezed her tighter. "You're okay. It's over." He buried his nose in her hair and simply breathed.

The whole fucked-up situation was wrong on so many levels, but this, holding this woman, felt like the only right thing in the world.

"Huh," an annoying voice said. "Looks like we wasted a trip. It seriously took you this long to protect your woman from *that*?" Ryan pointed at the mewling heap that was Ben.

Jake smacked the back of Ryan's head. His gaze scanned the area before flicking between Travis and Willow. "Are you okay?" he asked her.

She nodded, her cheek scraping against Travis's chest. "Thanks to him." She tilted her head to look up at Travis. "That was a big knife. I can't believe you just walked up to him and took it."

It had been a little more involved than that, but there was one thing that would never change. He cupped her cheek. "I will always put myself between you and danger. Always."

Her eyes glassed over. "God, I love you. I know you probably think that's the stress talking, since all I do is push you away, and I'm so sorry—"

He pressed his finger to her lips. "We'll talk later." When she wasn't riding high on adrenaline and emotion. But the way she was looking at him gave him hope. So much so that he replaced his finger with his mouth. The kiss was sweet, desperate, and tender. It was a promise, one he swore he'd never break.

Someone cleared his throat. "We are at a grade school," Tony said. "Let's keep this PG, One Shot."

Willow dropped down from her toes, breaking the kiss, breathless.

Travis glared at his friend. "There is a man who needs medical attention over there. Why don't you go help him?"

Tony wrinkled his nose. "I really don't want to touch that one. Besides, he's not bleeding out or anything."

"The police and an ambulance will be here soon." Chris shoved his phone in his pocket. "Hey, how about that fish restaurant that we never got to try for lunch? I hear their tacos are out of this world."

"You know I hate seafood," Tony grumbled.

"Why the hell did you join the Navy if you hate seafood?" Ryan shook his head. "You should have become a grunt."

"What does branch of service have to do with taste buds?" Chris joined the squabble.

Willow wrapped her arms around Travis's waist. "You just took down a man who wanted to kill me. Why are they talking about food?"

"They're idiots." But they were his idiots, and must have broken every speed law to get here so quickly. "After we give our statements to the police, can you get Tilda out of school? Lunch doesn't sound half bad." And he wanted to have it with his two girls. No, after seeing a man pointing a knife at Willow, he needed it.

She laid her cheek on his chest and melted into his body. "Sounds perfect."

Chapter Twenty-Five

WILLOW STOOD IN THE bedroom doorway, watching as Travis lay Tilda on the double bed in his guest bedroom. He pulled the covers up over her slack body and smoothed her hair away from her face.

Her heart fluttered so hard it was almost an ache. She'd forgotten how sweet it was to see a man caring for her daughter. She'd tried so hard to be everything to Tilda. And then she'd tried so hard to keep it that way, for some damned reason. She'd been a fool not to let someone else into their family. Not to let Travis in.

Travis strode toward her, a small smile dancing around his lips. "Wow, she really goes narcoleptic when you turn the TV on, doesn't she?"

Willow closed the door and headed back to the living room. She picked up the pillow Tilda had brought down to the floor and rearranged it back on the couch. "Only when it's getting near her bedtime."

Laughter broke out on Travis's back patio. After each of them gave their statements to the Swansboro PD, everyone had drifted back to Travis's townhouse for their own debriefing. Caroline and Sam had shown up after work, bearing Chinese take-out and brownies.

Willow really liked those women.

Travis wrapped his arm around her waist and pulled her up against him, so her back was pressed to his front. "How are you doing?" He rested his head against hers. "It's been so hectic I haven't gotten a chance to really ask. Especially since my house has somehow become Grand Central Station with my supposed friends."

She slapped his arm playfully. "Stop. There's nothing supposed about them. I still can't believe they all dropped everything when they saw Ben's phone was at Tilda's school and came running." And she couldn't believe Ryan had hacked into the phone's global positioning information. Having men like this on her side was surreal.

She shivered. If Travis had arrived only a couple of minutes later, what would have happened?

Travis tightened his arms. "You are okay, aren't you?"

She nodded. She still couldn't believe it was Ben who'd burned her building. Thrown a brick through her window. Pulled a knife on her. Frankly, she hadn't thought he was motivated enough even to seek revenge. But knowing who was behind all her trouble helped to quiet her fears. When it was some nameless enemy, it had been so much worse. "How much prison time do you think he will get?"

Travis stiffened behind her. "Not enough, but you don't have to worry. Whenever he gets out, I'll be ready for him."

She wasn't worried. Well, not overly so. Travis was more than a match for Ben Giles. "About this morning. About what I said." She bit her lip. He must think she was as flighty and temperamental as a teenage girl. First she wanted him, then she was pushing him away, then she was declaring her love.... It was enough to confuse any man. "I'd like to talk—"

"Do you have any ice cream?" Jake asked, coming through the sliding glass door to the patio. "Caroline is craving some."

"And some more beer." Tony followed him in. "The cooler is empty."

Travis made a deep grumbly sound that was absolutely adorable. "I'm sure there's beer and ice cream at one of your homes. Why don't you move the party there?"

Jake blinked, moved his gaze from Travis to Willow and back again, and nodded. "We'll wrap it up."

Tony was oblivious. "It's early yet." He disappeared into the kitchen. "Nothing but light beer," he shouted from the refrigerator, disgust tinging his voice. "I swear you eat and drink like a woman."

"If you don't like it, you can always go," Travis hinted.

Tony leaned against the door jamb and popped the top of the beer. "Naw, it will do." He took a swig. "I gotta say, Skee, if you get into trouble again, the drive to Swansboro sucks. We hated being so far away when you needed us."

"Who says I needed you?" Travis stepped to her side, his arm at her waist moving to her shoulders. "I handled the problem fine without you guys. I always thought our missions would go more smoothly if I went in solo."

"Why would Travis be in Swansboro?" She frowned. The odds of a situation like today happening again were astronomical.

Tony turned serious dark eyes on her. "I figure it won't be long before he moves down there. He won't want to live too far from you."

Jake groaned. "Viper, maybe leave that for them to talk over."

"It's okay," she said. "But you don't have to worry. I don't think I'll be going back to Swansboro."

The word 'really' echoed in the room, said almost simultaneously by Jake and Tony and followed by Travis's shocked exclamation. He turned her to face him, a question in his eyes.

She shrugged. "Without my store, the only thing keeping me there is Tilda's school. I'm sure the elementary schools are just as good in Jacksonville."

"You could rebuild," Travis said. "With someone arrested for the arson, the insurance company has to pay out."

"I can, but I don't think I want to." She'd loved her store, but with it gone, she felt like a burden had been lifted from her shoulders.

Jake grabbed Tony's arm and pulled him to the patio. "I'll go get Caroline, take her to that ice cream shop downtown. We'll go out the back gate and get out of your hair."

Travis nodded, but didn't take his eyes off of hers. "What do you want?"

She sank down onto the sofa, pulling Travis down with her. "So much it might scare you."

"Sweetness, I'm a Raider. I don't scare easy."

She looked down at their joined hands. "I've always wanted to write a cookbook, but I was too busy when I had the shop. And I still want to make jam, but I think I can make a living only selling online. They'll be no payroll, no unemployment insurance, no fire inspections." She grimaced. "I love cooking and baking, but running the shop took away from all that. Plus, I'll have so much more time for Tilda."

"That all sounds great." He tipped her chin up with the tip of his finger. "Anyone else you'll have more time for?"

She lifted one shoulder. "There is this one guy. He's been great, even if a little overbearing at times. I only hope he can forgive me for acting like a jackass?" Her palms went damp. Her brain knew by the way he looked at her that she didn't have to worry, but her stomach still clenched. She never wanted to take Travis for granted, and he'd be well within his rights to turn her down after she'd cut him off at the knees so many times.

"You were scared." He ran his thumb along her wrist, sending sparks down her spine to her core.

"Yes," she agreed. She'd been scared to take a chance on Travis, something that only felt more stupid by the second. Her daughter had been in a burning building. She'd faced down a man with a knife. That was fear. Travis had never given her a reason to doubt him. It had only been her own insecurities, her own anxieties, that had made her panicky. And it had been easier to be angry with Travis than face those fears head-on.

She swallowed. The pit in her stomach was partly due to shame. She hadn't been brave like Travis, like how she wanted Tilda to grow up to be. That was changing now.

"I knew I wanted you the moment I saw you," he said. The edges of his eyes wrinkled. "And I knew that was crazy, so I was willing to give you more time to catch up. Are we on the same page now?"

"Yes," she whispered. Same page, same book, same series.

Travis cupped her cheek and outlined her lips with his finger. His touch held everything in it.

She rested her hand on his thigh, needing to touch him, too. "So I thought I'd get an apartment for me and Tilda here in Jacksonville and start checking out schools."

He narrowed his eyes. "Is that what you thought?"

She leaned forward. "Unless you have another idea."

"You and Tilda will stay right here." It wasn't a suggestion.

As it was what she was hoping he'd say, she didn't mind. She hadn't wanted to look for a separate place, but it had felt crazy presumptuous to assume she and Tilda could just move in. "If you're sure." She skimmed her palm over his chest, up his neck, and dug her fingers in his hair.

"You'll move into the master bedroom. If you want to keep up proprieties in front of Tilda, I'll *sleep* on the couch until you're wearing my ring."

She paused, inches from his mouth. "Ring?"

"I started looking the week after I met you." He closed the distance and pressed his lips softly to hers. "I just didn't want to scare you."

She pulled herself up to straddle his lap. "This is the new and improved Willow Janna. I don't scare easy." To prove that fact, she fisted his hair and brought her mouth crashing down to capture his.

She kissed him with everything she had. Everything she was. She couldn't wait to wear this man's ring. Give Tilda a sister or brother with his child. She'd been living half a life until she met Travis. This time, she was jumping in with both feet.

He pulled back, out of breath. "So that's a yes?"

She nodded and dove back in. His cock hardened under her bottom, and she rubbed against it.

Travis wrapped her hair around his fist and pulled her back. "Yes to which question?"

Had there been actual questions? She grinned. "Yes to every-thing."

"'Bout damn time." He grabbed her waist, pivoted, and laid her on the couch. He hovered over her. His fingers slid under her T-shirt, moving steadily upward. "I can't wait to play house with you. I have this recurring fantasy of you in your apron, heels, and nothing else." He waggled his eyebrows. "How soon can we make that happen?"

She hooked her leg around his. He didn't seem in imminent danger of leaving, but she wanted to make sure. "There's no rush." She popped the button on his pants, eased the zipper down. She was done with rushing through life. Her new mission was to enjoy a slower speed, make sure she didn't miss a moment.

She'd lived too long without love, without passion. Not everyone got to have what she had with Travis. She wasn't going to waste it.

"This is just the beginning for us." She rubbed his erection through his boxers. Elation surged through her as he sucked in a breath, his gaze going hazy. She nipped his lower lip.

The backs of her eyes burned with happy tears. "You and me, we have forever." Forever with the man she loved. Life didn't get sweeter than that.

<<<<<>>>>>

Want more sexy Raiders? Sign up for Allyson's newsletter at ht tps://www.allysoncharles.com/newsletter-signup to be the first to know when book 4 hits stores!

About Allyson Charles

Allyson Charles lives in Colorado. She's the author of sexy and funny small-town romances, and steamy and fast-paced military romances. A former attorney, she happily ditched those suits and now works in her pajamas writing about men's briefs instead of legal briefs. When she's not writing, she's probably engaged in one of her favorite hobbies: napping, eating, or martial arts (That last one almost makes up for the first two, right?). One of Allyson's greatest sources of happiness is that she now lives in a city that has a Cracker Barrel.

Allyson Charles also writes steamy historical romances under the name Alyson Chase, and paranormal romances under the name A. Caprice.

You can find her at www.allysoncharles.com.

Printed in Great Britain
by Amazon

44930210R00106